Mark B. Mills has lived in both  and has written for the screen. Under the novel, *The Whaleboat House*, won best novel by a debut author. Hi was a Richard and Judy Summer His most recent novel, *The Long Shadow*, was publi 2013. He lives near Oxford with his wife and two children.

Praise for *Waiting for Doggo*:

'Prepare to fall in love!'   *Good Housekeeping*

'Mark B. Mills' new novel could well catch a new zeitgeist by recasting the lonely singleton of Bridget Jones infamy as a man'
Grazia

'It will take you about two sentences to fall in love with Doggo – and Dan won't be far behind. You'll be rooting for both of them . . . A heartwarming, funny and truly unique tale – don't miss it!' ★★★★★   *Heat*

'A witty and inspiring tale' ★★★★   *Closer*

'Fans of *Marley & Me* and *One Day* will love Mark B. Mills' new novel'   *Sunday Express*, S Magazine

'I wolfed it down . . . please say there's a sequel' Jill Mansell

'A wonderfully comic and feel-good read'   *Image* Magazine

'[An] emotionally rich storyline that you can believe in . . . there's much to like here'   *Irish Examiner*

'A must read'   *Woman and Home*

By Mark Mills

The Whaleboat House
The Savage Garden
The Information Officer
House Of The Hanged
The Long Shadow
Waiting For Doggo

WAITING FOR DOGGO

MARK B. MILLS

headline
review

First published in Great Britain in 2014 by HEADLINE REVIEW
An imprint of HEADLINE PUBLISHING GROUP

First published in paperback in 2015 by Headline Review
An imprint of HEADLINE PUBLISHING GROUP

1

Cataloguing in Publication Data is available from the British Library

ISBN 978 1 4722 1833 9

Typeset in Bembo MT Std by Palimpsest Book Production Ltd, Falkirk, Stirlingshire

Printed and bound in Great Britain by Clays Ltd, St Ives plc

Headline's policy is to use papers that are natural, renewable and recyclable products
and made from wood grown in sustainable forests. The logging and manufacturing
processes are expected to conform to the environmental regulations of
the country of origin.

HEADLINE PUBLISHING GROUP
An Hachette UK Company
Carmelite House
50 Victoria Embankment
London EC4Y 0DZ

www.headline.co.uk
www.hachette.co.uk

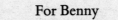

For Benny

Sing like no one's listening, love like you've never been hurt, dance like nobody's watching, and live like it's heaven on earth.
Mark Twain (1875)

Chapter One

DEAR DANIEL,
    God, that sounds so formal. I don't mean it like that, or maybe I do. As with a lot of things, I'm not sure any more/anymore (which one is it? I know you'd know). Shit, I'd start this letter again, but I've done that three times already and I'm late for my flight.

I'm going away, a long way away. I can't tell you where. Part of me wants to but there's no point because I don't know how long I'll be there. Anyway, it's better like this. That's crap, of course. What I mean is it's better for me like this, not for you, although I know you'll cope because you're strong and sensible and slightly cold-hearted.

We'll talk properly soon, when I'm feeling up to it, which I'm not right now, obviously, or I wouldn't be running away to Austral— Oops! (Joke. You see, I haven't lost my sense of humour like you told me the other night.) Okay, not funny under the circumstances. I can see you standing at the table reading this. I'm sorry, my dear darling Daniel. I'm a coward. At least I've learned that about myself. And I'm sorry about Doggo. That's totally my fault. God knows what I was thinking. What <u>was</u> I thinking? That he would make a difference, even heal us. You'll hate that word, like you hate it when I talk about journeys and energies and, yes, angels.

The thing is, I DO believe in them. And you don't. Is that what this is really about? Maybe. I used to love your polite tolerance, the sceptical smile in your eyes, but now it pisses me off. It looks cynical and superior to me now, like you think you have all the answers. Well, you don't. Who does? Maybe that's what you have to learn about yourself, like I've learned that I'm a coward. Maybe I can only be with a man who believes in angels. Don't worry, that doesn't mean I've run away with Brendon. Brendon's a prick. I'd take you over him any day (and if that's not a compliment, what is, right!?). No, I'm on my own, travelling light, following my nose. There's no one else, just me and you-know-who – the 'One Who Must Not Be Named', as you jokingly call him. I know you think he's a figment of my warped imagination, but I believe he's here with me right now, watching over me, and you can't deny that that feeling is real (even if you are right about angels, which you aren't!).

Take Doggo back. Something tells me you're going to get this job and you can't leave him shut up in the flat all day. It wouldn't be fair on him, and it's not like the two of you have hit it off. Is he there right now, peering up at you with those weird eyes of his? I swear he looked at me with a kind of contempt when I was packing my suitcase before, like he knew what I was doing. Of course he didn't, he's just a dog, a small, ugly dog. No, not exactly ugly, but you know what I mean – not overloaded with good looks, poor thing. I think I must have felt sorry for him when I first saw him. I feel bad about messing with his life, but at least he's had a change of scene, a short holiday. I would have taken him back myself but there wasn't time. You see, I haven't been planning this thing, it just came to me very suddenly. I saw what I had to do and I'm doing it.

Am I making the biggest mistake of my life? I don't think so. I think we got to a place where we were about to make a decision that would have been wrong for us, definitely wrong for me, and probably for you too. Don't hate me, Daniel. You'll feel humiliated, of course, but it could be worse. It's not like I'm leaving you standing at that altar, plus everyone will damn me as a bitch, which will make it easier for you. Please don't try and find me, and there's no point in calling me now because I'll be in the air by the time you read this.

Love and light

Clara XXXXXXXXX

PS I've just read this through and I realise I haven't made myself clear. It's over between us, at least for now, which I suspect means for ever, but who knows? Never say never, right? I need to feel open to other opportunities (yes, okay, other men). I can't stop you doing what you want to do, but if you sleep with Polly I'll kill you. She's young, vulnerable and in awe of you, but she's also my baby sister, so 'non toccare', as they say in Italy (reminds me of that gift shop in Lucca where you bought me a horrid china figurine of the Virgin Mary because you thought it looked like my father in drag). X

I lay the letter carefully on the table with a trembling hand. Cold-hearted? Really? Cynical and superior?

I never felt superior. It was our little game. We worked out the rules together. Astrology, past lives, guardian angels, whatever it was, Clara fell hard and I applied the brakes. We agreed to differ and we laughed along together because what we had was bigger than any of it. What we had was love. We agreed on that. She can't just change the rules and get on a plane and disappear after four years. It's my life too.

I want to be angry but it won't come. Stung by the accusations levelled against me, I'm also numbed by a cold, creeping sensation that I may in fact be guilty as charged.

I glance down at my feet. Doggo was there before; he's now on the sofa. He knows he's not allowed on the sofa, but he doesn't seem too worried about my reaction. In fact he's not even looking at me. His chin is on his paws and he's staring intently out of the window, as though the passing clouds hold the key to some metaphysical conundrum he's wrestling with.

'Doggo.'

He doesn't turn, but then again it's not a name he has ever answered to, possibly because he knows it's not really a name, just something we're calling him until we've decided what we're really going to call him.

We've tried everything – we've even trawled through websites of baby names, but somehow none of them fitted. For a while we thought 'Eustace' might be the answer. It didn't even last a day. According to Wikipedia, St Eustace was a Roman general who converted to Christianity only to suffer a grim catalogue of torments and misfortunes which included being roasted alive, along with his sons, inside a bronze statue of a bull. You had to hand it to the Emperor Hadrian: he not only knew how to build a wall, he had a dark imagination when it came to disposing of his enemies. St Eustace, I now know, is the patron saint of firefighters (the ones who failed to put out the flames that cooked him) and, more generally, anyone facing adversity.

'Eustace,' I say. 'I'm facing adversity.'

Doggo cocks his ear, just the one, the left one, but it's little more than a momentary twitch. His eyes remain fixed on the scudding clouds.

I pull my mobile from my pocket. I know her number is stored in it because we communicated about the surprise birthday party for Clara back in April. She works as a coordinator for a children's activities company and seems to spend most of her time white-water rafting in Wales. What with it being the school holidays, I'm expecting to leave a message.

She answers on the fourth ring. 'Daniel . . . . . .'

Just one word, but it carries in it an enticing mix of pleasure, surprise and anticipation.

'Hey, Polly.' Another twitch of Doggo's ear, the right one this time. 'How's it going?'

Clara only has herself to blame, I tell myself, almost believing it. The thought would never have occurred to me if she hadn't brought it up.

'Great,' chirps Polly. 'Working like a dog.'

I look at Doggo welded to the sofa, almost at one with it, and I wonder where on earth that phrase came from.

Chapter Two

IT ONLY OCCURS to me as we're boarding the bus.

'Am I allowed to travel with a dog?'

'Driver's discretion, mate.'

They're caged off nowadays, bus drivers, for their own protection, and he has to press his nose to the Perspex screen to get a better view of Doggo down below.

'Jesus,' he mutters, unimpressed. 'You'll have to have him on your lap.'

'I can't. He'll bite me if I try and pick him up.'

'What, violent, is he? A public hazard?'

'No, no, it's just that . . .' I trail off pathetically. What can I say? It's true: he will bite me if I try and lift him on to my lap.

'Sorry, mate, rules is rules.' Please don't say it, I think, but he does. 'It's more than my job's worth.'

Normally I would plead my case, even create a scene, but I'm not feeling up to it today. I was barely able to boil an egg for my breakfast earlier. 'Fair enough. Sorry to bother you. Have a nice day.'

I'm stepping off the bus when the driver says, 'Now if he

was a guide dog, say, or a seizure alert dog, or a mental health companion dog . . .'

'He isn't.'

The driver rolls his eyes and spells it out slowly for the dim-witted: "Cos all them dogs trump driver's discretion.'

'Oh yes, he's a seizure alert dog.' I pat my chest to make the point.

'Heart trouble at your age?' he snorts. 'You're havin' a laugh.'

But he's the one having a laugh at my expense. He winks, nods for me to take a seat. I touch my Oyster card to the reader and thank him.

'Tuck him out of sight. Don't want him scaring the other passengers, do we?'

This time he isn't joking.

The Battersea Dogs & Cats Home is jammed in between an old gasworks and the desolate wasteland that rings the long-defunct Battersea Power Station. It's hard to imagine a more miserable spot for the housing of unwanted pets. The tight triangular site is bordered by railway lines on two sides and a busy road on the other. The place has received a makeover since I last passed by it some years ago. (I rarely come south of the river; north-west London has always been my stomping ground, for no other reason than it's where I first landed in the capital.) A building with a curved glass facade now presents its gleaming face to the road. The flashy architecture seems a little excessive, a cruel taunt to all the expectant relatives who found themselves without a bean when the lawyer read out the terms of Great-Aunt Mabel's last will and testament. Unlike France or Italy, where there are rules and rightful percentages for descendants, you're free to shaft your family from beyond the grave in England, and animal welfare is often the winner in the legacy battle.

Doggo doesn't appear to recognise the place. He trips merrily inside, apparently oblivious to the dim but distinct yapping of dogs above the rattle of a passing train.

I explain my predicament to a woman at the front desk. She's as bright and cheery as the reception area where she spends her day, even when she tells me I really should have phoned ahead and made an appointment. It's probably just me, but I sense something brittle in the kindly smile that Laura (it's on her badge) flashes me. It brings to mind the carers at the grim nursing home near Brighton where my grandfather is seeing out his days. Is it really possible for someone to be so relentlessly good-natured? Or do they revert to true type once the front door has swung shut behind you, swearing like troopers and brutalising the unfortunates in their charge? So much for my resolution to rein in the cynicism Clara accused me of.

Ten minutes later, Doggo and I find ourselves in a cheerless office with another breezy young woman wearing a standard-issue polo shirt. This one is called Beth. She's a 're-homer', and she's clearly not pleased about having to re-home a dog that was homed only three weeks ago. It's a relief to know she's human. Beth is my sort of age, I guess, late twenties, and she leans forward, elbows on her desk, as she listens attentively to my story.

I play it for sympathy: how it was my girlfriend who wanted a dog, how she didn't even consult me but just turned up with it one day, how she then upped and left me with no warning.

I am not, I explain contritely, in a position to look after a dog on my own. Beth nods, but I can see her eyes searching my face for clues to the failings that drove poor Clara to flee me. I can see her wondering if I'm a violent man, or just boring. I don't care what she thinks, so long as she takes Doggo back and allows me to move on with my life.

I produce the buff envelope that Clara left out for me, the one containing the official paperwork. Beth doesn't require it; she has her own file. She didn't know Doggo but she's happy to process his 're-admission to the facility'. It's beginning to sound a little too George Orwell for my tastes, but I grin and thank her.

It turns out that Doggo was known to them as Mikey. Clara never mentioned it to me, but I can forgive her this omission. Mikey!? It would be like Winston Churchill's parents changing their minds at the last moment and deciding to call their bouncing baby boy Brian. I mean, would Roosevelt and Stalin even have sat down with him at Yalta if he'd been called Brian?

Beth frowns as she reads on. 'Strange, he was only with us a week before your girlfriend picked him out.'

'So?'

'I'd have had him down as a lifer.'

'A lifer?'

'Like in prison . . . here for the long haul.'

'Why do you say that?'

'Well, I mean, look at him.'

I look at Doggo, but there's not much to see. He has folded back on himself and is licking his balls.

'That's not right,' says Beth.

'Doggo, stop it.'

'No, I mean we have a neutering policy here.' Beth flips through the file, finds what she's looking for. 'Ah, okay. He wasn't here for long enough. Your girlfriend undertook to have it done.'

This time I correct her. 'My ex-girlfriend.'

'Whatever. She signed here to say she'd have him seen to.'

'Seen to?'

'Snip snip.'

I flinch. Maybe you have to be male to understand that castration can't be reduced to finger-scissors and some onomatopoeia.

'She never said.'

Beth lays her palm on the sacred file. 'It's here in black and white.'

But it isn't black and white. No, it's grey, very grey. We're talking about Doggo's balls.

'I need to think about this.'

'It has to be done.'

'Why?'

'Because it's policy.'

If she knew me better, she wouldn't have said it.

'It was Nazi policy to exterminate Jews, gypsies and homosexuals. Did that make it okay?'

Beth looks deeply affronted; she even gives a little gasp. 'I really don't think that's fair.' Her eyes have a sudden watery sheen to them and I look away out of awkwardness. Doggo is still lapping away. I can't remember ever having seen him so happy, and I find myself rising to my feet and extending my hand across the desk.

'Beth, it's been a pleasure, but Doggo and I are leaving now.'

★

It's pathetic on my part. He's just a dog, a dog I never wanted in the first place, but I'm expecting gratitude, or something. A glance to acknowledge the two-legged animal at the other end of the lead would do, but I don't even get that as we make off down the road towards Battersea Park.

'Hey, pal, they were going to chop your bollocks off.'

Doggo stops to sniff the base of a litter bin.

'That's right. Snip snip. *Adios testiculos*. Your bloody bollocks – gone.'

My timing couldn't be worse. I'm so focused on Doggo, wondering if he's about cock his leg and piss against the bin, that I don't notice the children in dinky blue uniforms disgorging from the school, not until one of their well-heeled mothers exclaims, 'Excuse *me*! Language!'

I know the type: blonde and painfully thin and sure of her place in her privileged world. Just like my sister. I'm tempted to retaliate when I see her young son cringing with embarrassment at his mother's intervention.

'My apologies, young man.'

'What's his name?' the boy asks unexpectedly.

'Doggo.'

There's an enormous 4X4 illegally parked nearby, two wheels on the kerb, its hazard lights flashing. The woman zaps it with her key fob. 'Hector, come along now.'

Hector's a beautiful boy, like the young Christian Bale in *Empire of the Sun* – all floppy hair and large green eyes. 'Hey, Doggo,' he coos warmly, dropping to his haunches.

Doggo doesn't just tilt his head at Hector, he allows the boy to stroke him, to rub his ears and scratch beneath his chin.

'Aren't you the best dog? Yes you are, Doggo. You're the best dog ever.'

'Hector!' comes his mother's indignant cry.

The boy glances up at me and rolls his eyes. 'Got to go.'

'It gets better – life, I mean.'

'Let's hope so,' he says. 'See you around, Doggo.'

The two of us stand and stare as Hector clambers into the back of the big Mercedes. He gives a wave as the car pulls away.

Let's hope so? And delivered with the weary forbearance of a biblical sage. He can't have been more than twelve years old. Where did this child come from? Not from his mother, that much is certain.

I follow Hector's lead and drop to my haunches. 'Hey, Doggo, you just made a friend.'

As I reach out a hand, I wonder at first if it's the sound of the passing traffic I can hear, but it's the low rumble of a warning growl telling me to keep my distance.

Chapter Three

'Can I say it?'

'I don't know, J, can you?'

'I'm going to anyway.'

I spread my hands. 'Sock it to me.'

We're in a bar on the Portobello Road, and J throws back a slug of his third (or is it his fourth?) mojito before coming out with it. 'You're well rid of her, mate.'

'Clara?'

'Who else? I never liked her.'

I'm shocked. 'I've been with her almost four years. You don't think you could have told me before now?'

'Grow the fuck up, Dan. I'm seriously going to tell you the love of your life is loopy as a box of frogs? Jesus, I'm not that stupid. What, have that one come back and bite me in the arse when you tie the knot with the loon?'

'She's not a loon.'

'She's certifiable, mate, always was. Hey, don't get me wrong. It was fine when we were younger, but this is life now, the real deal. We're looking at the long game. I mean, take Jethro, for example.'

'What about him?'

'His time is over.'

'Jethro?'

Jethro is the coolest guy we know. Tall and artfully dishev-elled, he divides his time between dossing on other people's floors, smoking huge quantities of weed and playing his guitar (rather well). He's like some latter-day troubadour, always on the move, forever searching out a new patron to house and feed him.

'I'm telling you, that guy's currency is in serious freefall. All women like a bad boy when they're younger, but let's face it, Jethro isn't the bloke you want bouncing your firstborn on his knee. He'd probably drop the bloody thing on its head.'

'I like Jethro.' I really do. He's got a great sense of humour and he can tell stories like no one else I know.

'Hey, me too,' soothes J. 'But he's had his day. Women our age don't want a layabout, however charming, not when the old biological clock starts ticking.'

He's right. It's the reason Jethro's girlfriends are getting younger. Poor Jethro.

'Clara's nothing like Jethro.'

'All I'm saying is I can see why you went for her. She's hot, hot as hell, and a bit crazy, which is okay when you're young, but we're not any more . . . sorry to break it to you. You really want a wife who's into crystals and auras and fuck knows what else?'

'Angels.'

'Angels!?'

'She met a bloke called Brendon who persuaded her she's got a guardian angel.'

'You're having me on!'

'His name's Kamael.'

A look of vacant incredulity falls across J's face. 'I rest my case.'

J and I met at Warwick University, where we both studied English. It's one of those rare and rather special friendships (more common between men than women, in my experience) where two people utterly unlike each other in character and temperament hit it off. I tend to come at life cautiously, grateful for whatever it bestows on me; J attacks it as if it were an assault course, every hurdle and impediment tailored to slow his progress. He has the energy, drive and ambition of ten men, possibly a hundred.

There's common ground between us, of course. At Warwick, it was our passion for literature. We blathered on for endless hours about how we would carve out careers for ourselves in publishing. Publishing needed people like us — young minds in tune with the digital revolution that was just starting to shake up the industry. We figured we would have to go our separate ways to begin with, but only in order to learn the ropes. At the first opportunity, we'd set up our own outfit together, build it into a multimillion-pound business and flog it off to the highest bidder.

Well, we both sold out long before then, J accepting a job offer from McKinsey during our last term at Warwick, and me winning a place at the D&AD Graduate Academy soon after. A management consultant and an ad man: that's what we've become. Talk about derelict dreams.

I sometimes console myself with the thought that at least

I make my living from words, but the truth is, I produce pithy straplines for companies I care next to nothing about. I'm a copywriter, and not a bad one. There are some hideous awards trophies gathering dust in my airing cupboard to prove it. Things were better before Trev ('Fat Trev', as he once insisted on being called, though no longer) had his breakdown. He was my art director. We work closely together, copywriters and art directors. It's a creative partnership, a team of two. We even move jobs together. I knew Trev was a depressive; it's why he was such good fun to work with. I guess I should have seen it coming, even alerted someone, but the thing is, he was producing his best ever stuff when the proverbial straw broke the camel's back. He's okay now. Only okay, mind. The meds have stripped him of everything that once made him him. There are no rough edges left, no highs, no lows, and certainly no laughs, but at least he's alive. It turned out he was thinking of swallow-diving off the block of flats he lives in near Bermondsey.

Maybe Clara's right, maybe I'm cold-hearted, but I can't help smiling whenever that image comes to mind: Fat Trev swallow-diving. It's something to do with the comic coupling of bulk and dainty finesse, like that ballet-dancing hippo in Disney's *Fantasia*, the one prancing around in a diaphanous tutu. I hope that one day I'll be able to share this thought with Trev and have a good giggle about it. Meanwhile, though, I'm on my own.

It hasn't been easy. I've been wandering in the wilderness for almost six months now, eating into my savings, fretting about mortgage payments. No one wants a lone copywriter. I've still got enough of a name to wangle a meeting or two with the people who were our rivals for those hideous trophies. Mostly, though, they're just curious to meet me and get the first-hand dirt on Fat Trev.

Indology might be different. I'll know soon enough.

'Indology?' scoffs J. 'What kind of name is that for an ad agency?'

'Not a bad one,' I counter, defensively.

We've moved on to another bar by now. They've gone for a post-apocalyptic look: raw brickwork and rough concrete and industrial steel lamps, which might or might not be the next big thing in interior design.

'They're small, new, independent.'

'Okay,' J concedes. 'I get the Ind—, but the –ology . . . ?'

'It suggests a kind of method, a rigour. Like psychology, theology, sociology—'

'Wankology.'

'Apparently they ran it past the focus group but it got a thumbs-down.'

J laughs and grips my arm. 'Sorry. I hope it comes to something, I really do. When's the interview?'

'Day after tomorrow.'

J has to close his eyes to make the calculation. 'Thursday. I'm in Frankfurt. Ever been?'

'Frankfurt?'

'Don't bother, it's a shithole. Good people, though, the Germans. I've got a lot of time for the Germans.'

That heartens me. J is from German-Jewish stock and lost a bunch of his family three generations back. He knows the stories – they were fed to him with his mother's milk – and yet he's still prepared to bury the hatchet and move on. His largesse makes me feel much better about the far more trifling matter of being dumped by the woman I thought I was going to marry.

Chapter Four

I REMEMBER WHAT BETH said at the dogs home (with a misting of pity in her eyes): 'I mean, look at him'. But the truth is, I've never really looked at him, never sat and scrutinised him as I'm doing now.

Clara was right – he *is* small and, in spite of her efforts to pretend otherwise, he *is* ugly. I didn't actually grow up with dogs, but I know them, they were a feature of my life from an early age. By and large, though, they were big dogs, dogs that could fill a room with their boisterous, panting presence: retrievers and Labradors and setters. These were the dogs my grandfather loved, far more, I suspect, than he ever loved (or even liked) my grandmother. That said, she's the one left looking after Hecuba – a colossal, neurotic Bernese Mountain Dog – while my grandfather slowly fades from life in his horrible rest home.

Doggo couldn't be more different from a Bernese Mountain Dog. He is everything a Bernese Mountain Dog doesn't wish to be. He is tiny, white and almost entirely hairless. I say almost, because there are tufts of hair here and there, wild patches, like the bits of a lawn a lazy gardener has failed to mow. There's a strip of shagginess along his spine, and a touch of the same at the tip of his thin tail. There are also tight curls – not brown, not yellow, but something in between – at the back of his forelegs. They suggest a dose of spaniel, as do the three neat forelocks of the same colour (piss, possibly). The snout is all wrong for a spaniel, though. It's too stumpy, too pug-like. It hints at something Oriental, like a Pekinese. No, it defies any obvious categorisation. It suggests a dog who has careered headlong into a brick wall then chosen not to have corrective surgery. There's a droopy, somnambulant quality to his eyes that reminds me of a bloodhound, but the eyes themselves are lively and alert. Right now, though, they are pinning me to my chair with a cold and searching steadiness.

Does he know what I'm thinking? Does he know I'm wondering whether his front haunches are so much more developed than the hind ones because his head is too big for his body and the muscles have to work overtime?

He blinks lazily from the sofa.

He has adopted the sofa as his own over the past couple of days, and out of sympathy (for the loss of his mistress) I haven't fought him on it. He liked Clara. He perked up in her company, as we all did.

'Where is she, Doggo?'

No one knows. Not Fiona, not Hatty, not any of her good girlfriends. Unless they're all lying to me. Part of me wants to indulge the paranoia, steep myself in the conspiracy of it, but I'm pretty sure Polly was being honest when I spoke to her earlier and she told me the family still hasn't heard a peep out of Clara. Apparently their parents are tearing their hair out.

Polly and I have spoken three times since her sister hopped on a plane and disappeared. We've exchanged many more texts than that. I might have been the first to add a kiss to the end of one of them, but it was Polly who doubled it, then tripled it. I've kept pace with her, matching her every time. At this rate we'll be up to xxxxxx by the end of the week. There are probably rules about such things, codes known only to a select band of initiates. Maybe xxxxxx means 'I'm happy to have you do y to me'.

$6x=y$

It strikes me that if x is 4 (the number of years Clara and I have been together), then y is Polly's age, which happens to be six years younger than I am. There's a pleasing circularity to the equation, although it's poor justification for where my mind is really taking me.

I guessed right: Polly is indeed in Wales, where the white-water rafting is better than ever after the recent downpours. She's driving up to London on Saturday with a vanload of kids, heading back on Sunday with a fresh bunch of the little shits (her words, not mine). I've already booked the restaurant where we're having dinner. It's a great little Italian place, intimate but buzzy, just a few minutes' walk from my flat. I popped in there earlier to choose the table, and I've just texted Polly to say that if she can't face the cab ride back to the flat she shares in east London then she's welcome to crash at my place. I signed off with only one x, which I figured was a decorous way of saying: no, not like that.

It *is* my place. Clara officially moved in with me about a year ago, but mine is the only name on the deeds. Her flat, way to the west beyond Acton, is rented out, and a portion of the proceeds goes towards my mortgage every month. Not any more, I now know, because I checked last night – the day her money usually lands in my bank account – and I saw that it hadn't. That shows foresight, a certain degree of planning. For all her apparent skittishness, Clara can be surprisingly pragmatic.

A thought occurs to me. I check the mail I've allowed to pile up unattended on the side table in the hall since she left. There's not one letter addressed to Clara, even among the junk. Going online, I discover that there's a lead time of five working days for the Post Office's redirection service.

The forensic eye I've just trained on Doggo begins to spot things it hasn't before now, things like the gaps in the book-shelves and the CD stack, and the missing cushion on the armchair, the cushion she bought in Cornwall last Easter. A minute later I'm on my knees in the kitchen, checking the cupboards. The wooden salad bowl we haggled over at a street market in Bungay is no longer there, neither is the Magimix. I've pictured her hefting a couple of armfuls of her clothes into a waiting car, but we're starting to talk serious volume now: packing cases and at least two trips in a car, and questions of storage. The stuff in her letter about it being a knee-jerk impulse to bolt seems less likely with every cupboard I open.

I'm strangely relieved. Impulsive departure suggests a degree of sudden revulsion – 'Oh God, I can't take it any more' – whereas a planned exodus, however upsetting in its own way, allows you to share in the reasoned thinking that informed it. I can see why she left. Of course I can, because I've felt like doing it myself a couple of times. She beat me to it, though, and with a brutal panache that almost makes me feel proud of her. How sick is that?

Truly sick, says Doggo's look.

He has abandoned his precious sofa and crept up on me. I'm still on my knees in front of the kitchen cupboards, so we're almost eye to eye. Am I wrong? He now seems to be regarding me with something that trembles between pity and disdain.

We see what we want to see, I remind myself. I'm obviously suffering from a case of the Kuleshov effect. The great Russian film-maker proved it almost a century ago with his montage of an actor gazing at a bowl of soup, then at a dead girl in a coffin, then at a beautiful woman stretched out alluringly on a divan. Kuleshov's audience was blown away by the wildly divergent emotions the actor was able to bring to a blank stare – ravenous hunger, grief, and sexual desire – until Kuleshov revealed that the footage of the actor was identical in every instance. They simply saw what they wanted to see. They brought their own expectations to the table.

That's what I'm seeing now: myself, rendered abject by my sleuthing, reflected back at me in Doggo's black and slightly bulbous eyes. He probably just wants a Choc Drop. He knows they live in the cupboard under the kitchen sink.

'Who wants a Choc Drop?' I say, in that weird way you do to dogs and small children.

He wags his tail.

Chapter Five

IT'S AN UNPREPOSSESSING entrance, a grey door at the far end of a cobbled yard in the heart of Soho. There's an intercom on the wall and a nameplate that reads: INDOLOGY.

Beyond the grey door, an industrial steel staircase climbs to a spacious reception area. They've gone for an enigmatic look, nothing overtly corporate or self-congratulatory (like framed awards certificates on the walls), nothing that can define or date them. An attractive young brunette with a pixie crop and geeky glasses looks up from her computer. I told her my name when she buzzed me in, and she clearly knows why I'm here.

'They'll be with you shortly. Grab a seat. Can I get you something to drink?' She's well-spoken and she has shrewd blue eyes.

'A coffee would be great.'

'What kind? We do all kinds.'

'Small, strong and black, please.'

'Double espresso?'

'Single.'

'You're hired,' she jokes.

I like her already. I like her more when she rises, rounds

her desk and offers me her hand. 'I'm Edith.' It's a name from another era. It suggests parents with an interest in odd and arcane things.

I've been kicking around in the business long enough to know that it's people like Edith who will one day be running outfits like this. They're not professional receptionists; they take what they can, anything for a foot in the door. They're smart and, above all, patient. In Edith's case, the long levers and gamine looks won't hinder her rise through the ranks.

'It's Colombian,' she says when she returns with my coffee.

'And if *they* don't know about drugs, who does?'

I fear at first I've overdone it with my reply, but she smiles. 'You should have said. We have Coke, too . . . normal and Diet.'

Yep, she's going all the way.

I've never met Ralph Aitken before, but I've seen him across a crowded room at a Christmas drinks party thrown by some agency or other a couple of years back. He's hard to miss, even at a distance, and not because he's unusually tall. Like me, he barely nudges six feet in his socks, but there's a presence about him, a loud and avuncular energy that challenges you to match him if you can (while threatening to destroy you if you dare). He has cornered the market in back-slapping bonhomie and he really doesn't want any pretenders to the throne. He has a full head of close-cropped silver hair, a well-developed tan and jeans that are far too tight for any self-respecting sixty-year-old. There's also an estuarial clip to his accent that suggests a man who has pulled himself up by his bootstraps.

I know that Indology is the third agency he has founded, and that the sale of the first two has made him a rich man, probably rich enough to retire. I also know that I need him to offer me a job, so I'm more than happy to worship at the altar. The other man seated at the big oval table in the conference room is wearing a jacket, a sure-fire sign that he doesn't head up the creative team.

'Tristan Hague,' he says, only half rising from his chair to shake my hand. He's effortlessly handsome, and something in his smile suggests he knows it. Something in the way he utters his name suggests I'm supposed to recognise it. I know what he means; it does ring a dim bell.

'Tristan is our MD,' explains Ralph. 'He joined us from *Campaign* a few months ago.' *Campaign* is the industry magazine, a confection of news and incestuous gossip that I hardly ever read. Nonetheless, it's coming back now . . . Tristan Hague . . . the pithy opinion pieces with their whiff of satire (and slight smugness?).

'*The* Tristan Hague?' I ask.

This pleases him greatly and he shapes a winning smile. 'Poacher turned gamekeeper.'

'Or gamekeeper turned poacher, if you prefer,' adds Ralph.

Ralph, I'm beginning to understand, is a good audience for his own jokes. He's also the boss, so we both chuckle indulgently, Tristan and I, briefly united by our subservience. This being England, we're talking about the inclement weather when Edith appears with the coffees. I notice there are four cups on the tray. The fourth one turns out to be for her, and she settles down with it to the right of Ralph. She can't be here to minute the meeting because she doesn't have a pad with her.

'I've asked Edith to sit in,' explains Ralph. 'I hope you don't mind.'

'Of course not.'

'You'll see why.' He doesn't elaborate; he plants his elbows on the table, interlaces his fingers and says, 'So, tell us about Fat Trev.'

I wasn't lying, I like Fat Trev, but I'm sick of being quizzed about him, probably because I know that if I was the one who'd gone doolally, then Fat Trev would not be sitting where I'm sitting right now being quizzed about me. Fat Trev is a legend, a 'character', larger than life, and I'm seen as the silent partner, the comedy fall guy, the Stan Laurel to his Oliver Hardy. I know the truth is far from that, that Trev was *my* sounding board, the touchstone against which I tested *my* ideas. No one likes to have a myth punctured, though, and I've learned to tell it as others want to hear it: me, the safe pair of hands, crafting the crazy outpourings of Trev's hare-brained genius into something vaguely presentable.

'And you can spare us the modesty,' Ralph adds.

This throws me. 'Sorry?'

'What Ralph means,' Tristan weighs in, 'is that we've asked around . . . people in the know . . . and it seems Fat Trev was pretty good at stealing your thunder.'

I'm not quite sure why I'm here. They were the ones who contacted me, suggesting I come in for a chat. I've brought my 'book' with me – the bound folder with samples of my work – but they show no interest in it. They spend the next ten minutes telling me about themselves, about Indology, where they're at, where they're going, how they plan to get there. Tristan does most of the talking. His conversation is peppered with irritating phrases like 'panning for creative gold', 'taking the battle to the marketplace' and 'turning traditional tropes on their head', but he trumps the lot of them when he suddenly announces, 'We're all about zagging while others zig.'

Think of the job, I tell myself. *Do not laugh. Hold his eye and nod sagely.*

Either they like blowing their own trumpet to anyone who'll listen, or they're selling themselves to me. I'm daring to believe it's the latter when Ralph slides a file across the table towards me and my heart sinks.

'This is a new product launch, another mouthwash from our old friends at KP and G.' Apparently market research has shown that the public is ready for something less medical when it comes to mouthwashes. They've had their fill of gum disease and plaque control; they're open to a new approach. The brief is for an eye-catching nationwide poster campaign. They're calling it SWOSH!,' says Tristan. 'Note the cheeky little exclamation mark.'

It's an old trick, one I've fallen foul of before. The job is the bait they dangle to draw out some free ideas. Pissed off that I've been dragged across town under false pretences, I resolve to give them nothing, or at least play my cards very close.

Annoyingly, I'm impressed. They've gone for a series of black-and-white shots of couples in clinches, though nothing as mannered as Robert Doisneau's famous kiss. The images have a more sultry quality than that, as though sex is only moments away, or even happening as we watch. They're all different, as kisses are – in one, the woman is cradling the man's face in her hands, confident, assertive – but they are united by the same strapline: 'Embrace Life'.

'They're good,' I say.

'But?' says Ralph.

'But nothing.'

'Nothing at all?' demands Tristan. He glances at Ralph, who glances at Edith, who is examining me with a curiously intense look. And only now does it make sense. They're hers, Edith's. That's why she's sitting in on the meeting.

'I don't believe you,' she says. 'Something's wrong.'

She's right, and I flick through the folder another time, but only because it's her and I like her. 'Maybe they lack a bit of impact.'

'Impact?' comes back the chorus.

I've vowed to stay silent but I can't stop myself. 'The images are great, but I'm not sure there's quite enough tension between them and the strapline. It's like they spring from the same place.'

'And what's wrong with that?' asks Tristan, a little too aggressively.

'Marcel Duchamp stuck a urinal on the wall of an art gallery and called it "Fountain". Would it have worked as well if he'd called it "Urinal"?'

Ralph smiles. 'Go on.'

No more freebies, I think. 'That's it.' I remember being in Edith's shoes; I remember the terror in the early days of putting my work out there for all to see and pick apart, and I make a point of turning to her. 'Well done.'

She nods her thanks, but it's not convincing. She looks crestfallen. Ralph requests a moment alone with me, and although Tristan is clearly reluctant to leave the room, even surprised that he should be asked to do so, he and Edith make themselves scarce. Ralph waits for the door to swing shut behind them.

'You're right, even if they think you're wrong.' He sits back in his chair and grins at me. 'Marcel Duchamp. I like that. I wish I'd said that.'

'You will, Oscar, you will.'

He laughs. 'Why haven't we worked together before?'

'You couldn't afford me.'

He laughs some more. 'What makes you think I can now?'

'The Bentley with the personalised number plate parked in the courtyard.'

It's weird, I don't normally talk like this. Fat Trev talks like this (while I look on, smiling coyly). I'm not sure how long I can go on channelling Trev, but fortunately I don't have to. Ralph slaps his hands down on the table and announces, 'Okay, here's the deal. Sixty grand basic, plus a bonus based on business won. You get medical and a company pension, although personally I wouldn't touch the pension with a bargepole. Those bastards in the City will have figured a way to pay out peanuts by the time you get to retire.'

I'm stunned. I've completely misjudged the situation, and it's a great package. I'd have taken a lot less.

'You'll be working with Edith, bringing her on, blooding her. She's wet behind the ears, but quick as a whippet. She needs someone with experience to play off. You think you can do it, train her up for the big time?'

It's an appealing thought; I just have one question.

'What's your policy on bringing pets to work?'

'Easy. No one does.'

'I have a dog, a dog I can't leave at home.'

Ralph has a habit of running his fingers through his hair, as if checking that it's all still there, which, remarkably for a man his age, it is. 'Deal-breaker?'

I shrug apologetically. 'Sorry.'

'What kind of dog?'

'Hard to say.'

'Big, small, medium?'

'Small.'

'Potty-trained? It's not going to crap everywhere, is it?'

'No.'

Ralph stands and thrusts his hand across the table. 'Tristan's going to kill me, but what the hell.'

Chapter Six

I'T'S ONE OF the funniest things I've ever seen, and Polly was right there beside me when it happened, shoulder to shoulder, our skis planted perpendicular to the plunging fall line of that evil slope.

It's called the Tortin – a forty-five-degree scoop out of the mountain round the back of Verbier. We never intended to ski it, but we missed the last lift up to the easy run home to our rented apartment in Nendaz and found ourselves with no other choice. There's a long traverse across the top that requires a heart-stopping near-sheer drop into the piste. You keep traversing, hoping it will somehow level out. It doesn't. All that happens is that the moguls waiting for you at the foot of the drop become bigger, like VW Beetles covered in snow. Only that year it wasn't snow, it was ice. They hadn't had a dump in weeks.

Clara's the best skier of the bunch by a mile. I'm rubbish. I've always been rubbish. Polly runs Clara a close second, and Polly's boyfriend, a hulking South African called Jannie, is almost as crap as I am. The other couple – Martin and Miranda – are competent. It makes no difference. The Tortin levels us.

We go over the lip one by one and we all fall, sprawling, spinning, sliding away. We dust ourselves down, recover our skis and stare down the piste. Have I ever been more terrified in all my life?

Clara leads the way, a snaking, controlled skid through the monster moguls that Martin and Miranda do their best to emulate. Polly hangs back, sweetly concerned for Jannie and me. Jannie's not a man accustomed to sweet concern from women – he's a big Boer hunter-gatherer type – and he grows increasingly irritable, more so when he sees me getting to grips with the descent. Complaining of cramp in his calves, he dumps himself on his arse and orders us to go on ahead; he'll catch us up.

Some distance down the slope, Polly slides to a halt ahead of me. 'I think we should wait for him.'

The light is fading fast and Jannie is a dark smudge on the mountainside. Polly waves. Jannie doesn't wave back. He forces himself to his feet with his poles and hollers down to us in his tight 'Sarth Ifrican' brogue: 'It's all in the mind. You have to be brave, attack it, get the chest down the slope. You have to believe.'

Ten seconds later, when he passes us, he's airborne and travelling at an incredible lick. He's also upside down, perfectly inverted.

'Fuck me,' he says, just before his head clips the top of a mogul.

We managed to get him to laugh about it later, and Polly and I are laughing about it now in the restaurant.

'Oh God,' she gasps. 'Poor Jannie. I'm not sure his ego ever recovered.'

We're both in a good mood. Polly is enjoying a welcome blast of city life after a month in the back of beyond, and we downed the best part of a bottle of champagne in my flat earlier to celebrate my new job. I imagine we'll polish it off later. Polly has taken me up on my offer of staying the night. Right now, her holdall is sitting on my bed. It's hers – the bed, I mean; I'm taking the sofa. I made that perfectly clear. Doggo will have to find somewhere else to sleep, such as the stupidly overpriced spongy dog basket Clara bought him and which he has barely glanced at since she left.

We talk about her, inevitably, although she doesn't crop up in conversation until we're well into our main courses. Polly has a hunch she's in Bali. I can see it. Clara has always been fascinated by Bali. She was heavily into Hinduism before switching to Buddhism, and the island is stuffed with Hindu temples. I wonder how her guardian angel will take to the place. Will Kamael fit right in, or will he sulk? Is there any place in Hinduism for angels? I make a mental note to look it up on the Web later.

The other thing Bali has going for it as a likely destination for Clara is artistic communities. She'd be right at home with a bunch of painters, potters, stone-carvers and silversmiths. She's a freelance stylist for TV commercials – it's how we first met – but the job description doesn't do justice to her creativity. She's always doing things with her hands: sketching, painting, making her own jewellery and clothes. Secretly I hope she's answering some call deep within herself, because that would explain her behaviour while exonerating me. When I mention this to Polly, she scoffs.

'She's flighty. She always has been, even when we were kids. Flighty and self-absorbed.'

'You think?'

'It's always been about her. I mean, what kind of person just disappears without a word to anyone? It's infantile.' She waggles her hands in the air. 'Look at me, look at me . . . only you can't because I've gone away and I'm not telling you where.'

I know Polly and Clara have their issues – what siblings don't? – but I've never had any inkling before now that Polly held her elder sister in such low regard.

'Honestly, Dan, I'm amazed you've put up with it for so long. You're very understanding.'

'Or just weak.'

'You're not weak. That's the last thing you are.'

Clara wrote in her letter that Polly was in awe of me. I dismissed it at the time as ridiculous, but there's a glimmer in Polly's brown eyes that suggests something close enough. *Don't*, I tell myself. *You mustn't*.

'What's the first thing?' I ask.

'Funny. You've always made me laugh.'

'And the second?'

'Hey, enough about you,' she says, reaching for her wine glass. 'Tell me about me.'

It's not inevitable. In fact I've done everything to make it evitable, like laying out my sleeping bag on the sofa and setting the alarm for Polly in the bedroom and suggesting she use the bathroom first. She blows away the theatre as soon as she's done brushing her teeth.

'I can go to bed and you can go to bed and then I'll just have to wait a bit before coming through to the living room

35

and asking if you want to join me. And that's okay, I'm happy to, even if you don't want to – join me, I mean – but if you do, well, it seems like a waste of precious time, seeing as I've got to get up early in the morning . . .'

She's standing there in front of me, coy and unbearably cute in a white T-shirt.

'Clara said she'd kill me if I slept with you.'

'You believe her?'

'I think she meant it figuratively.'

'She'll never know.' Polly holds up her right hand, the thumb and little finger bent and touching. 'Brownie promise.'

'You were never a Brownie.'

'I *so* was. Just not a very good one.'

'No, a very bad one indeed – a rotten little Brownie.'

Polly smiles and takes a step towards me. 'Put it this way, if it doesn't happen now, it's never going to.' She reaches for my hand. 'Can you live with that? Because I'm not sure I can.'

If Clara is the arty one of the pair, Polly is the sporty one. She played county hockey for Hampshire when she was younger. I don't know what I'm expecting, maybe something athletic, vigorous, possibly a bit mechanical. I couldn't be more wrong. She's like liquid in bed, like treacle, unhurried. I have to fight not to drown in her. If it's revenge, it's the sweetest revenge I've ever taken, and it leaves no place for comparisons. She's so utterly unlike Clara, so at ease with herself.

Clara gets a mention afterwards. 'She walked away from that? She's mad.' Polly licks my damp neck, then whispers in my ear, 'I feel like the cat that got the cream.'

'So to speak.'

She's on top of me and I'm still inside her, so when she laughs, I feel it too.

It's a parody of a dog turd – perfectly coiled and rising to a point, like some plastic replica you'd buy in a joke shop. It's waiting for me right outside the bedroom door when I go to make us tea in the morning.

In the half-light bleeding through the venetian blinds, I can see Doggo curled up on the sofa. I know he's faking, pretending to be asleep.

'Message received,' I mutter as I shuffle past him towards the kitchen.

Nothing. Not even an ear twitch. Damn, he's good. And the Oscar for Best Sleeping Dog goes to . . .

Chapter Seven

IT'S MY FIRST day at work, and there's a definite spring in my step as we weave through the streets of Soho. Doggo seems to sense my mood, scampering merrily along beside me.

'Stop,' I command, as we make to cross Broadwick Street. He doesn't, not till the lead snaps taut. 'Remember what we said? Right, left, right again.' He looks at me like I'm mad. I crouch down beside him, pointing. 'Right. Left. Right again.' Amazingly, his eyes actually follow my finger.

'Oh my God, that's so cute!'

Two overweight girls in high heels are teetering along the pavement towards us.

'What?' asks her friend. 'Creepy guy talking to creepy dog?'

The taunting cackle of their laughter fades away towards Wardour Street.

'Don't worry about them,' I say to Doggo. 'They're what we call—'

I bite my tongue. I'm not sure I should be teaching him bad words.

*

It's a morning of introductions. First there's a gathering of the whole company in the conference room, all twenty or so employees. Ralph makes a speech and I smile awkwardly, then everybody goes back to work. Phase Two involves me making the rounds with Tristan and Edith (not forgetting Doggo, who carries himself as though the whole thing has been laid on for his benefit and he's not quite sure yet whether he approves of his new colleagues).

We get a frosty reception from Margaret in Accounts.

'She has a cat,' Tristan offers by way of explanation once we've moved on.

'So?' asks Edith.

'Well, she now wants to know why she can't bring it to work too.' His tone leaves little room for doubt about where he stands on the question of Doggo.

The Indology offices occupy two sides of the courtyard. There are skylights in the pitched roof, stripped boards on the floor, and all the furniture is designer minimalist. The effect is calming, coupled with an air of brisk, no-nonsense efficiency. There's a lot of spare space. 'Plenty of room for growth,' says Tristan. 'And we're all about growth.' Ralph cut his teeth in the industry back in the 1970s and doesn't hold much truck with the open-plan ethos of modern office design. The account executives and the planners all have their own private offices. Tristan approves. 'When you're smarming a client, the last thing you want is other people eavesdropping on your bullshit.' I'm not sure if he's joking.

The pitch for the SWOSH! campaign is being handled by Patrick Stubbs. Patrick is my age, maybe a couple of years older. He's a skinny fellow with an engagingly bookish look about him. I glimpse a framed photo on his desk of a younger man, blond and lantern-jawed.

'There's a lot of good feeling towards us at KP and G,' says Patrick. 'If we win this one, who knows what else they'll bung our way? I guess in the end it comes down to you two.' He means Edith and me, and he says it with an ironic twinkle that implies: so, no pressure or anything.

'We're on it,' says Edith.

'So's everyone else,' cuts in Tristan. 'We need you all over it.'

Edith looks stung by his words, the unnecessary reprimand. We all know time is tight and there's a lot riding on it.

'Oh, I think we can stretch to all over, don't you?' I say to Edith.

'Yeah, I reckon,' she replies quietly.

The creative department consists of a run of offices centred on a large games room of the kind often found in creative departments. There's a pool table (naturally) and table football and a darts board and a couple of other activities which, over the years, the 'creatives' have somehow managed to convince the 'suits' are vital for the free flow of ideas. I love shooting pool (especially in office hours, when I'm being paid to do so), but the truth is, I've never had one half-good idea come to me while racking the balls or lining up a shot. They usually clobber me on the back of the head while I'm standing in a queue at the supermarket, or cycling home from football under the Westway on a Thursday evening, or emptying the dishwasher. Never when or where you expect the muse to strike – that seems to be the rule for me.

'You play pool?' Tristan asks.

I'm not a fool. 'I've had some of my best ideas while playing pool.'

'Edith doesn't.'

'Of course she does,' I say. 'She just doesn't know it yet.'

There are two other creative teams. I've been where they're at right now, and I know what they're thinking. For all their smiles and their words of welcome, no one likes a new face around the place, let alone two. Edith and I are the enemy, potential rivals for the choicest accounts.

'I loved your work on spreadable butter.'

His name's Seth, and I can't help thinking it's a backhanded compliment, especially when he quotes me the strapline: 'Quickly Does It'.

Not exactly my finest hour, although better than Fat Trev's suggestion at the time: 'You Can Hardly Taste the 25% Vegetable Oil That Makes the Fucking Stuff Spreadable'.

Seth is teamed with Megan, an Australian art director, tall, shock-headed and loud. 'Great to have you guys on board. What's the dishlicker called?'

'Doggo. It's temporary.'

'What is he?' She has obviously spotted his balls.

'I don't know.'

'Didn't it say on his pedigree certificate?' This from Connor, a lank-haired and bestubbled Irishman, who is rewarded with a sudden fierce glare from Doggo. 'Jesus, does he understand English?'

'Of course he bloody doesn't,' says Clive, Connor's art director partner. 'He just knows an Irish windbag when he sees one.'

My first-impression rankings go like this: Clive in the top

spot; Megan second; Seth third; Connor bringing up the rear. Megan almost immediately drops two places when she asks, 'Remind me, why do we have to have a dog in the office?'

'It was a condition of Daniel signing with us.' Tristan shoots me a glance that says: over to you. It's fair enough. He doesn't know. No one knows.

'He was my girlfriend's dog.'

The use of the past tense (plus the intimation that my girlfriend is no longer in a position to look after said dog) sets them all wondering if some terrible mishap has befallen her – cancer maybe, or a car accident. No one is brave enough to ask.

Doggo seems more than happy with his new office. Someone has furnished it with a long leather sofa just for him. He tests it out, approvingly. The room overlooks the courtyard and is large enough for two desks separated by Doggo's sofa. It's a great space. I can see myself working happily and fruitfully in it. Edith has tentatively set up shop down the far end. I remind myself that this is a big step for her – from the desk in reception to one tucked away in the furthest reaches of the building. She doesn't yet feel entitled to be here. It's probably the reason she has been so silent up until now; she's wondering if the other creatives will ever accept the receptionist as one of their own. The answer is simple: not before she wins her spurs with some quality work, which by default will also threaten them.

'Don't worry about them,' I say, once we're alone.

Edith gives a dismissive shrug. 'I'm not.'

'Well you should be. There's no such thing as a happy family, especially in a company this small.'

Edith's shoulders sag and the pretence goes out of her. 'Oh

God,' she groans. 'This is supposed to be the happiest day of my professional life so far. I had my mother on the phone this morning in tears – tears of joy. She's even googled you.'

'*Moi?*'

'I mean, I don't know what we're supposed to do. How do you work? What did you do with Fat Trev?'

'Flick bits of paper at each other, mostly, but our desks were much closer together. We might have to go for rubber bands.'

'You *are* a long way away.'

'That's easily remedied.'

An hour later, we have totally rearranged the office. Our desks are now almost side by side, both directly in front of the windows overlooking the courtyard, and the sofa (plus Doggo) has been shifted to fill the space vacated by Edith's desk. These changes may appear trivial, but they're *our* changes. We now possess the place in a way we didn't before, and I trap the moment for posterity with a photo on my phone.

'What now?' she asks.

'Lunch, of course. My shout.'

It's a restaurant I know on Lexington Street, a bit on the gloomy side unless you happen to get one of the four tin tables in the postage-stamp yard out back, which luckily we do.

Edith tells me to call her Edie. She wants to talk about work, and so do I, just not the stuff she means. I'm looking to get the low-down on Indology, the blood and guts, the friendships and rivalries, rumours, truths and half-truths. This is more than just lurid curiosity on my part. I know from hard experience that such details matter when it comes to picking the path of least resistance through a new organisation.

After almost a year on the front desk, Edie is a storehouse

of water-cooler gossip. I discover many things (not least of all that she prefers Chardonnay to Sauvignon Blanc, and that after a couple of glasses the cutest ghost of a flush brightens her long pale neck). The important revelations are these: that Megan and Seth had been struggling for a while with the SWOSH! poster campaign when Edie first mentioned her idea about the black-and-white kisses to Patrick, who brought it to the attention of Tristan, who flagged it up to Ralph, who thought it was a great concept and told her to run with it. Patrick is regarded by Ralph as a good guy, smart and highly personable, but a little on the weak side, possibly not quite up to closing the big deals expected of a top account man. As for Tristan, one-time journalist, he muscled himself the position of managing director after bringing in some crucial financial backing (not his own). He's married to a lawyer, and they have a young son.

Edie seems very protective of him, which isn't so surprising when you consider that it was Tristan who championed her promotion from receptionist to budding new art director. Never bite the hand that feeds you, as the old adage goes. They're words I would also be wise to remember. It seems it was Tristan who suggested me as the perfect copywriter to partner Edie.

'He rates you very highly.'

I'm only human; I'll take the flattery, although somehow I can't see Tristan Hague having any interest in me or my work. Edie reads my expression correctly.

'Ask him if you don't believe me. Now, can we talk about the campaign? We can't go back to the office empty-handed.'

I won't be. I can now safely assume that Megan and Seth

want us to fail, that Tristan is keen for us to succeed, that Patrick needs us to succeed, and that Ralph ultimately calls the shots.

These are the bold brushstrokes. With time, I'm sure the more subtle shadings will fall into focus.

Chapter Eight

THERE'S THE RETURNING home to an empty flat at the end of the day, of course, but the worst thing is the weekends.

Even when Clara and I were stretched on the work front, we always made sure that Saturdays and Sundays remained sacrosanct. We also had a rule that once a month we would drive off somewhere for a night in our clapped-out little Peugeot. (Ours? Mine. Still mine.) It was always a surprise for one or other of us, a guessing game for the person in the passenger seat until we finally pulled to a halt in the car park of some far-flung pub or hotel.

I took Clara to Ely, out in the Cambridgeshire fens (or what used to be the fens before they drained the wetlands for pasture), and to Studland Bay on the Dorset coast, and to see *Twelfth Night* in Stratford-upon-Avon. She introduced me to the Neolithic standing stones of Avebury Ring and the thermal waters of Bath, and to paragliding (in a shallow bowl scooped out of the Surrey Downs). Less successfully, I also took her to watch Portsmouth play Southampton in the fifth round of the FA Cup.

Are these meaningless memories? Am I completely deluded? J isn't the only friend of mine to share an opinion on Clara since she jetted off to God knows where (although I'm not sure even He knows). Many of the others have let slip in various ways that they found her a bit of a handful, that we weren't good for each other. I wonder how long I can keep telling myself they're wrong, that the best of what we were was known only to us.

Polly texted me yesterday, even though we vowed not to communicate for a couple of weeks: *Why aren't I feeling more guilty? X*

Because you have no moral rudder, you hussy x

LOL. God I miss you. Sorry, I shouldn't say that x

Might be flattered if you weren't in, er, Wales x

It's not so bad x

Liar x

I can remember every delicious detail of that night. Damn, there I go again. Don't worry, have to dash. Middle-class brats screaming for burgers and yours truly on BBQ duty xx

Rereading the exchange later, it strikes me that Clara and I would never have been able to produce it, that anything we wrote would have been bogged down in an earnestness of her or my making. The alchemy with Polly is a law unto itself, a wild beast prowling through the undergrowth. I'm seriously tempted to pick the conversation up where we left off. In the end, though, I take Doggo out for his final dump of the day.

I love where I live. My flat is on Chesterton Road, which is a continuation of Golbourne Road, which lies at the top end of the Portobello Road. It's not quite Notting Hill, but in my opinion it's all the better for it. The area has an edgy, front-line feel to it, although long-term residents probably think it has been gentrified out of all existence by yuppie ad men like me moving in. Either way, it's still a rich mix of North Africa and Portugal, designer boutiques and junk shops, hardware stores and specialist bike shops for people who could buy a motorcycle for the same money. The whole thing is overlooked by that soaring testament to 1960s brutalist architecture, Trellick Tower, which stands sentinel at the northern end of Golbourne Road.

This is my stomping ground. I've been here for three years now and I can't imagine living anywhere else. I love it more than ever, even on Saturdays, when the whole world descends on the street market and the hordes of visitors spill from the pavements into the streets. Doggo, I sense, is coming to love it too, if only because the Moroccan chefs sneaking cigarettes out the back of their restaurants toss him scraps of food when we make our evening pilgrimage to Athlone Gardens. Athlone Gardens is Doggo's latrine, the place where he dutifully craps and I dutifully bag it up.

In American romantic comedies, owning a dog is a sure-fire way of bumping into cute girls before bedding them. You meet them in Central Park (maybe their dog tries to mount your dog – a bit of canine gender reversal to take the edge off the obvious parallel); you part on awkward terms, resolving to keep your distance from each other in the future so as to avoid a repeat of the ugly spectacle, et cetera, et cetera, right through to the final scene in the church when, just as you're exchanging your marriage vows, her dog attempts to mount your dog once again (tee-hee).

In Kensington Gardens on a Sunday morning, most of the dog-owning women make my grandmother look like a spring chicken, and the few fit ones are, well, fit. You'd have to be an accomplished athlete to stand any chance of exchanging even a few words with them, that's how fast they run, their lanky pedigree hounds bounding along beside them.

You could never describe Doggo as a lanky hound. He's a stumpy, honest-to-God, salt-of-the-earth, deep-dyed, through-and-through mutt. Remarkably, he seems to have no sense of this whatsoever. It's something I've noted at the office over the past week or so. He holds himself like royalty, as though all eyes are on him and he can't afford to slip up for fear of disappointing the adoring crowds. Kensington Gardens, with its better breed of person and dog, is definitely his kind of place. He's at home here, in his element, so much so that I wonder if he doesn't know it already. On reflection, I'm not sure he does. For all his haughty self-assurance, he seems uncertain of his environment.

I've brought him here to stretch his legs, to let him run properly free for the first time since Clara left. He's not interested. Yes, he wanders off to bury his snout in the base of a tree every so often, but he always keeps one eye on me. I'm touched by the little glances; they suggest a reliance on me that I haven't felt before now (although it's quite possible he imagines he's the one in charge, and he's simply checking to see that I'm not getting up to any mischief).

It's a glorious, sunny, windblown May day, and I decide to treat us to a spin round the Serpentine in a rowing boat. Doggo hops fearlessly aboard and plants himself in the prow, paws on the gunwales, surveying the water like a captain from his poop deck. He seems as surprised as I am by the shiver in his hind haunches and the little whimpers he emits every time we near some ducks. I'm not sure he likes to think of himself as subject to the baser instincts that make other dogs tick.

Last night I came close to blowing out Sunday lunch with my sister. The moment she opens the door of her terraced house, I wish I had.

'Oh God,' she groans. 'A dog.'

I love Emma. Of course I do. She's the one who held it together when Mum and Dad split, the one who filled in for them when it came to me. It's just that I haven't seen her for five years, not the real her, not the person who would once have smothered me in a hug and made a joke about the rubbish bottle of red wine I've brought with me. For some reason, everything now has to be 'just so' in her life. Her brother turning up with a dog is an unexpected irritation, a detail she's struggling to factor in to the preordained vision of how the following few hours will unfold.

'Don't worry, he's almost house-trained.'

'Dan—'

'Joke, Ems.'

Emma and Duncan have two kids. Milo is a permanently disgruntled blob of a two-year-old, upstairs, sleeping, probably drugged with Calpol. Alice is six, downstairs and playing the piano in the kitchen cum dining room. She's the real reason I didn't blow out lunch.

'Who's making that God-awful racket? Oh, it's you.'

She spots me coming down the stairs. 'Uncle Dan!' She

drops off the piano stool, scampers over and throws her arms around my waist. 'What have you brung me?'

'Brought,' corrects Emma at my shoulder.

'What makes you think I've brung you anything?'

''Cos you always do. You're my godfather.' Her eyes widen at the sight of Doggo on the landing above. 'You brung me a dog!?'

'Brought,' says Emma. 'And it's Uncle Dan's dog.'

'He's called Doggo, unless you can come up with a better name.'

Alice thinks on it with a serious little face before deciding, 'It's a good name.'

I wince suddenly. 'Oof!' I pat the back pocket of my jeans and pull out the wrapped package with a puzzled look. 'What's this doing here?'

'It's for me, it's for me!'

It's a silver necklace.

'That's the symbol of peace,' I explain.

'Peace?'

'Because there's too much war and killing in the world.'

'Maybe you can show her some photos of mass slaughter on the Web,' calls Emma from the cooker.

'I love it,' beams Alice. 'Put it on me.'

Duncan is in the garden, flapping a bit of cardboard at the barbecue. 'Bloody charcoal's damp. It's been in the shed all winter. Good to see you.' He breaks off from his flapping to pump my hand.

He's a good man, Duncan, the sort of chap you'd want beside you in the trenches, the sort of chap to whom you could say, 'Duncan, old man, the Captain asked if I'd make a quick recce of no-man's-land but I've got the most dreadful headache.' Duncan would happily go in your place, return unscathed and probably earn himself a medal in the process. He's utterly unlike all of Emma's previous partners, the string of feckless young men who taught me to swear and smoke and listen to Bob Dylan when I was younger.

'Sorry to hear about you and Clara,' he says awkwardly. 'I'd have offered five to one on you'd go the distance.'

Duncan has always been a betting man. He sees life in probabilities. He doesn't gamble any more; Emma doesn't allow him to, except at work, where he trades bonds for an Italian bank.

'Maybe you still will,' he adds.

'Unlikely.'

I mean it. I've spent a couple of weeks feeling sorry for myself – confused, wounded, even vengeful – but I refuse to become one of those sorry fools who carries a guttering torch for someone who wants rid of them.

'Just took off, huh?' asks Duncan, a wistful look in his eyes. 'Still don't know where?'

'No.'

He goes back to his flapping. 'I rather liked her.'

'Really?'

'Absolutely. Well, mostly.'

'I'm sure she'd be touched to know you rather liked her mostly.'

As long as I've known Duncan, he has laughed like a bad actor performing to order. 'Ha ha ha,' he chortles stiffly. 'I could tell she wasn't always easy.' It's his polite way of saying she was several sandwiches short of a picnic.

I'm the first to arrive, but I'm not the only guest. There's a couple I've met a few times before, Hugo and Lucinda, as well as my date, Fran, who works as a research analyst at Duncan's bank. I'm assuming she's my date because she's my age (or close enough) and single. She's also sullen, chippy and caustic. She's rude about Doggo, dismissive of Islington (where we are all gathered), and she drops a snide comment about parents who drone on endlessly about their children. It's quite a feat, to alienate every person present within twenty minutes or so of arriving.

While Duncan fights to keep the butterflied leg of lamb from becoming a burnt offering, I find myself looking at Fran across the teak table in the garden and wondering what makes an intelligent person like her tick so out of time with everyone else. It's as if she's consciously committing social suicide. This makes her extremely intriguing, of course, but only because she's also extremely attractive. Without her looks, she'd be sitting alone at home right now.

When she takes a swipe at the middle-class obsession with organic food, it pops out of my mouth unbidden: 'Without your looks, you'd be sitting alone at home right now.'

'Dan!' chides Emma.

'Don't I know it,' says Fran, fixing me with an amused look. 'And thank you. That's the first honest thing I've heard since I got here.'

'There's more to life than honesty,' blusters Hugo.

Fran ignores him, her eyes still fastened on me. 'Say something else.'

'Quid pro quo.'

Fran drops another slice of salami into Doggo's mouth. 'Why did your girlfriend run away?'

'That's cheating.'

'You never said it couldn't be a question.'

'Okay,' I reply. 'Because I don't believe in angels.'

'Why not?'

'Because there's no evidence for them.'

'Ah, an empiricist. Maybe you're blind to the evidence. Maybe you're looking for halos and wings when you should be looking for other things.' She pauses briefly before adding, 'Maybe I'm an angel.'

I can't resist it. 'Great disguise.'

Fran laughs loudest of all.

Duncan keeps a fine cellar, and as the claret flows, Emma finally begins to relax. So does Fran. She has set out her stall – Hi, I'm Fran, your resident misanthrope – but she's smart enough to know that labouring the point would only be boorish. She even tells a sweet anecdote about a hedgehog and a garden broom that has us all in stitches.

I clear the plates away and find myself alone in the kitchen with Emma, who's dusting her home-made chocolate torte with icing sugar. 'Sorry about Fran. God only knows what Duncan was thinking.'

'I like her.'

'Then you must be worse off than I thought,' snorts Emma. I snaffle a raspberry from a bowl. 'Don't!' she snaps.

'Ems, it's a raspberry.'

'I knew I should have bought another punnet at the farmers' market.'

Not a line I ever thought I'd hear my sister utter.

'Two Our Fathers and two Hail Marys should cover it,' I say. We're lapsed Catholics, so it's okay to joke about such things. When Emma asks about the new job, I tell her the truth: that it's great to be working again, functioning, earning.

'So who have they got filling Fat Trev's shoes . . . sorry, open-toed sandals?'

'Her name's Edie, short for Edith.'

She throws me one of her knowing looks. 'Intriguing. Age?'

'Twenty-five.'

'Attractive?'

'Kind of.'

'Elaborate.'

I begin to describe Edie, then remember I have a photo of her on my phone, the one taken just after we'd finished re-arranging our office. She's posing in the middle of the room, smiling broadly, arms spread wide in a 'ta-dah' fashion.

'Kind of?' says Emma. 'She's bloody gorgeous. Bitch.'

Ah, there you are, I think. *Finally.*

I explain that she has a boyfriend, Douglas, and that they've been together for ever – well, since they met at Cambridge University.

'Cambridge? Did you tell her you tried to get in and failed?'

'Yes, Ems,' I reply wearily.

'Did you tell her I tried to get in and did?'

'Weirdly, you haven't come up in conversation yet.'

'It won't last. University relationships never do.'

I tell her it's never going to happen, Douglas or no Douglas. The thought of living and working with the same person fills me with a kind of cold terror. All day together, then nights too? Talk about cabin fever.

'I'd be climbing the walls within a week, looking for a way out. I know what I'm like.'

'So do I. You'll change your tune the second you fall in love with her.'

'I forgot, big sis always knows best.' I reach for another raspberry.

'Big sis says don't even think about it.'

Alice takes me aside as I'm leaving and tells me not to forget her birthday, which is coming up soon. She also has a question for me, a question she imagines only a godfather is equipped to answer. She wants to know if church steeples are shaped the way they are because they're really rockets for taking dead people to heaven. I hug her and tell her she's the smartest little god-daughter in all the world.

There are no lifts home to be had; Hugo and Lucinda live north, beyond Stoke Newington, so Fran walks with Doggo and me to Upper Street in search of a cab. Over the past couple of weeks I've found myself living life at one remove, almost as if I'm disembodied, floating above proceedings. Fran's plain speaking is refreshingly grounding; it leaves no place for floating.

'When Duncan invited me to Sunday lunch, I almost laughed.'

'Why?' I ask.

'Doggo knows, don't you, Doggo?' Doggo looks up at her. 'You see.'

'He's just had about a kilo of meat out of your hand; of course he's going to look at you.'

Fran gives an appreciative chuckle.

'So, why did you almost laugh?'

'Oh, because Duncan knows what a nightmare I can be.'

'Maybe he has a masochistic streak,' I suggest.

'Or a sadistic one.'

'Sadistic?'

'Come on, we both know why I was there.'

'Do we?'

'For you,' she says.

I don't answer immediately. 'That's very presumptuous. Maybe I was there for you.'

'Oh God,' she groans. 'I'm such a bloody narcissist, it didn't even occur to me.'

She lives near Earls Court, and it makes sense for us to share a cab, at least some of the way. Doggo and I find ourselves dropped off at Marble Arch, where Fran waves aside my offer of a tenner towards the fare. 'Don't be ridiculous. And just so you know, I definitely would.'

'What's that?'

She rolls her eyes. 'Use your imagination.'

'Ah well, I'll carry that thought with me.'

She's got a great smile when she chooses to use it. 'It's better this way. I'd only screw you over.'

'Why would you want to do that?'

'No idea. I'm working on it with my therapist.'

It's not the last thing she says to me.

'I've recently done to someone what your girlfriend did to you. Don't think she's having the time of her life, because she isn't.'

Chapter Nine

IT'S MEGAN'S IDEA and it couldn't come at a worse time. Something tells me she knows this.

Patrick is pitching to KP&G on Friday afternoon, which means that Edie and I need to have settled on a strapline by the end of play on Wednesday, because Josh and Eric in design need at least a day to mock some stuff up. The Sword of Damocles is hanging above our heads by a thread; the last thing we need right now is an office-wide competition to come up with a proper name for Doggo.

When Megan refuses to be deterred, I realise that I've underestimated her desire to see us crash and burn.

'Come on, guys, it'll be fun.' She says it standing in our office, with an irritating Aussie chirpiness designed to make us feel like Pommy stick-in-the-muds. I still can't say for sure whether Seth is in on it. 'Yeah,' he drawls from the doorway, in the spirit of someone who knows this is heading somewhere, just not where exactly.

It pisses me off that Doggo is being used against us, but as someone once wrote, it kicks open a door in the palace of possibilities.

'Let's do it,' I say suddenly, levering myself to my feet. 'Doggo, let's go find you a new name.'

I'm aware that Edie is looking at me as if I'm mad. Doggo, of course, doesn't move from the sofa. 'Give him a nudge, will you?' I say to Megan as casually as I can, making a show of shutting down my laptop. She claps her hands together. 'Come on, Doggo.' He doesn't react, so she tries to lift him off the sofa. That's when it happens.

'He bit me!' she howls, recoiling.

'Doggo! Bad Doggo!' I examine Megan's hand. 'It's just a nip. He didn't draw blood.'

'A nip!?' She skewers Doggo with a look. 'Little shit.'

'Maybe now's not the right time,' I suggest, ladling on just enough false courtesy for her to suspect I know exactly what she was up to. What can she say? She's been rumbled. She sucks at her hand and retreats, taking Seth with her.

I flop on to the sofa beside Doggo and slip him a Choc Drop.

'That can't be right,' says Edie.

'What's that?'

'He'll associate biting Megan with reward.'

'You reckon?'

When another Choc Drop disappears between Doggo's eager lips, she finally gets it. 'I had no idea you were so evil.'

'Self-defence, your honour. She started it.'

There are no rules in this game. It doesn't matter where it comes from, just so long as it comes. Unfortunately, it isn't right now.

Edie and I have chewed it over and over. Some of the ideas

aren't bad, but none of them quite makes the grade. Even Ralph, supremely confident in our ability to crack it, is beginning to have his doubts. He summons a war council in his office.

'I know there's nothing to be gained from me cracking the whip.'

'But get your bloody skates on,' adds Tristan, joking – well, sort of.

We're all agreed that the images work brilliantly. They're mysterious, eye-catching, quietly erotic. Full credit for them goes to Edie. They weren't bought in from some photo library; she art-directed the shoots herself. She has an eye, the all-important eye. I don't have it, although I've learned to recognise it when I see it in others. Edie has somehow managed to make mouthwash sexy. More importantly, she has associated the product with that most universal of pleasures – the human kiss. Who doesn't love a kiss? Okay, maybe nuns don't go a bundle on them, but nuns aren't our target market.

Only the strapline is missing. The best of the bunch so far is: 'Just Say No'. It works well with the sensual images, playing to the idea that forces beyond your control will be unleashed in you if you wash your mouth out with the stuff, but Patrick feels there's something a tad too knowing about the conceit, piggybacking, as it definitely does, on Nike's iconic 'Just Do It'. Ralph holds even firmer views on the subject. He's convinced that the line should include the name of the product. Since he's the boss, so it shall be. We've got forty-eight hours to figure it out.

My default position at times of pressure is one of breezy optimism, whereas Edie likes to tackle stress head-on, wrestling it to the ground with a wild animal cry. I know this works for some people, just as I understand that my laid-back attitude can be infuriating to those who don't share it.

'For God's sake, Dan.'

'What?'

'Do you think you can stop playing sudoku on your bloody iPhone?'

'Sshhhh.'

I'm playing live against someone who calls herself Madame Butterfly, and I've decided in my mind that if I beat her (although 'she' is quite possibly a hairy Bulgarian mechanic, such is the way of the world nowadays), then everything will be okay for Edie and me – we'll come up with a killer line and win the account. There are probably better ways to ensure success, but it's the test I've set myself and I have to see it through.

Madame Butterfly pips me to the post.

'Shit.'

'What?'

'She beat me.'

'Who?'

'Madame Butterfly.'

Edie shakes her head. 'I'm beginning to understand why Fat Trev went off the deep end.'

It's early days, we're still feeling each other out, but I already know that I like Edie a lot. She's smart, funny, ambitious and hard-working. That's not all, though. She gives off something else, much harder to define. It's to do with the way she fills the space she occupies. There's a poise about her, a lazy grace, a quiet dignity. Sharing an office with her is like sitting at the base of a large tree (whereas sharing an office with Fat Trev was like standing in the mosh pit at a thrash metal concert).

She definitely brightens my day. I look forward to seeing her each morning, and I feel a twinge of emptiness the moment we part company at Oxford Circus at the end of every day, she for the Victoria Line south to Pimlico, Doggo and me for the number 23 bus back to Ladbroke Grove.

Madame Butterfly calls for a rematch, but I kill the phone and turn to Edie. 'Let's get out of here. We need a change of scene.'

I'm amazed more people aren't wise to it. I mean, why queue for hours and hand over good money in order to fight your way round the latest okay offering from the Royal Academy or Tate Modern when some of the finest art in the world can be viewed for free at the major auction houses? Whatever your tastes, Christie's, Sotheby's and Bonhams hold an endless round of sales to satisfy them, everything from Ancient Egyptian through to Chinese Contemporary. My personal favourite is Post-War European (although Old Master Drawings also gets me going).

The big sales, the ones that make the headlines, are Impressionist & Modern, because that's where the silly money is spent. Last year in New York, Sotheby's sold an Edvard Munch pastel of *The Scream* for a staggering seventy-four million pounds. I seriously thought about getting on a plane in the days leading up to the auction. The picture had been in private hands pretty much since it was painted, and in all likelihood would disappear once more into a private collection (which it duly did). For the briefest of moments, though, it was available for all to see; you simply had to walk in off the street and stand in front of it. It's gone now, not for good, hopefully, but I'd be surprised if it resurfaces before I'm dead. Last time, it lay tucked out of sight for over a hundred years.

That's the thing about auctions: you brush with beauty of all kinds, but the encounters are fleeting, transitory, never to be repeated – like catching the eye of a gorgeous woman you pass in the street.

I don't mention any of this to Edie as I usher her inside Christie's on King Street. A man in a black uniform moves to intercept us. 'I'm sorry, sir – guide dogs only.'

'He is a mental health companion dog.' It's a line I've had to use a couple of times on buses, the voice a mild variation on my trainspotter/computer geek voice.

'A mental health companion dog?' He glances at Edie, who gives him a sweet and mildly concerned look. 'Well, I'm sure that's fine,' he says. 'Go ahead.'

It's a great sale, probably the most impressive I've ever viewed. I know what to expect because I've checked out the online catalogue. Among the forty or so lots there are three Renoirs, five Picassos, two Matisses, a Van Gogh, as well as a couple of Giacometti bronzes. Some of the star pieces are strangely disappointing (you can never really tell from the catalogue). Conversely, there's a landscape by Bonnard that looked flat and featureless on my laptop, but in the flesh it shimmers with the heat of a Mediterranean afternoon. You can almost hear the cicadas.

I always feel a touch of sadness whenever I stand in front of a Van Gogh painting. It's not just the crazed genius of the man, or his early death at his own hand; it's knowing that he went to his grave with no sense of the extraordinary impact he would have on the art world. Only a handful of his contemporaries understood that he was a visionary, a prophet.

The picture for sale is a small oil on canvas of the French asylum near Saint-Rémy where he spent some time. A swirling feast of blues, violets and oranges, it is estimated to sell for between ten and twelve million pounds. It's an absurd sum when you consider that he barely earned enough to feed himself during his own lifetime.

Edie, who I'm coming to understand has a contrary streak, disagrees with me, although there's a playful edge to the counter-argument she puts forward: that when all is said and done, we're just a pile of bones and a reputation. Maybe Van Gogh understood this; maybe he knew it was better to die at the height of his genius than as a bloke who had mastered his depression and then gone on to produce less good work for another forty years. 'It's like Steffi Graf.'

'Steffi Graf?'

'She was a tennis player.'

'I know who Steffi Graf is.'

'Steffi understood. She got out at the top of her game: I'm the best, thank you and goodbye.'

'Maybe it was her in-depth knowledge of Van Gogh's oeuvre that informed her decision.'

'If that's all you've got to say, then I've won the argument.'

'What argument? Van Gogh did not kill himself to secure his reputation for all of time.'

'Ah, but you don't know that. He might have.'

Edie clearly knows a lot about art but is happy to wear her learning lightly. When I push her, it emerges that she grew up in a cultured, bookish household, the only child of a composer cum music journalist father and a potter cum amateur archaeologist mother. They were always dragging her off to exhibitions and concerts when she was younger. J is the same: he was exposed to culture of all kinds from an early age, absorbing it by osmosis. I'm secretly envious of such people. There was never much of that sort of thing for Emma and me when we were growing up.

'My dad's a left-wing academic of the old school. He saw music and art as bourgeois fripperies. Maybe less so now.'

'And your mother?' asks Edie.

'My dad's not a man you stand up to, not if you know what's good for you.'

This wasn't the plan, to bleat on about my childhood, and I'm not exactly sure how it happened. The idea was to stick the two of us in front of some great art, because great art sets one's own sad stabs at creativity in proper perspective; it brings distance and clarity. Sometimes it even throws up solutions to problems.

Not today. Well, not immediately. Not until we're strolling back to the office along Piccadilly and I suggest to Edie that maybe we'll have to make do with 'Just Say No' as a strapline.

'I've gone right off it,' she says forcefully. 'It sounds too much like a government health warning.'

I know the sensation; it's always the same – a chill running across my shoulders. 'That's it!'

'What?'

'Clever girl.'

'What?' demands Edie. 'What did I say?'

★

It looks great mocked up. We wanted more tension between the image and the strapline and we've got it. A white strip cuts a crude swathe along the bottom of the photo of the kiss, and stamped across it in bold black letters are the words 'WARNING: SWOSH! CAN SERIOUSLY AFFECT YOUR SOCIAL LIFE'.

Ralph is delighted, and not only because we've managed to get the product name in there. He finds it daring, arresting, and he thinks the humorous little swipe at our health-and-safety-obsessed society has broad appeal. Moreover, it's a line that lends itself to variations. We shove a few in front of him. The one he likes most is 'SMOKING KILLS. SWOSH! DOESN'T'. It's not for now; it's for way down the road as the campaign evolves. Clients love a concept with legs; they feel like they're getting more for their money.

Ralph sits back in his chair. 'I love it. I'd pitch it myself if I didn't know Patrick was going to make it fly.' And if that isn't a warning shot across Patrick's bows, I don't know what is.

When we return to our office, Edie seems a little shell-shocked. 'Tristan didn't say much.'

'What's to say?'

'He's always got something to say.'

'Maybe he hates the idea,' I suggest.

'You think?' She glances at me from the sofa, where she is distractedly stroking Doggo.

'He's a pragmatist; he's probably just keeping his powder dry.'

'Meaning?'

Meaning why the hell are we talking about Tristan when

we've just received the kind of endorsement we could only have dreamed of from the main man?

'Don't worry about Tristan. Worry about how Patrick's going to perform on Friday. There's no medal for coming second.'

It's a big account and we're a small agency. The buzz soon builds. Clive and Connor are the first to stop by our office. They seem genuinely impressed with the work and pleased for us. Megan and Seth are almost as convincing.

'Great line, you bastard,' jokes Megan.

'Actually, it was Edie's idea.'

'Not really,' says Edie.

Megan bares her big teeth. 'You guys have really got to get your story straight.'

My only worry is that the concept might be a bit risqué. I don't say this to Edie. I tell her that even if it doesn't come off, she has made her mark on Ralph, which is just as important. 'Anyway, it would be sickening if you found a home for your first piece of work. It took me five attempts, and in the end it was a magazine ad for hearing aids: "Going Deaf? Buy One of These".'

She laughs, then says, 'Thanks for before. You know I don't deserve any credit for the line.'

'You were the one who said it: government health warning.'

'I said it but I didn't see it. You saw it.'

'Only because you spoke the words. Listen, what's mine is yours . . . ours. It's called teamwork.'

She doesn't reply immediately. 'You know, Dan, you're one of the good guys.'

I'm touched by the level of feeling in her voice. 'Tell that to Clara.'

It's a terrible line, dripping with self-pity, and the timing couldn't be worse, because when Edie asks, 'Who's Polly?' I stupidly assume the question is somehow part of the same conversation.

'Clara's sister. Why?'

I realise too late that I'm using the speaker dock on Edie's desk to recharge my iPhone, and an incoming text has just popped up right in front of her.

'Because she really needs to feel you inside her again.'

I squirm, searching for a reply. 'Like you said – one of the good guys.'

We're still laughing when Tristan suddenly appears in our office.

'Want to share it?'

'Definitely not,' I reply.

'Now I'm intrigued.'

I can see Edie wavering under Tristan's viper-eyed glare. 'Don't you dare,' I warn her. She shrugs apologetically to Tristan.

'As you like, children,' he says with a tight smile. 'I just wanted to say great job. Whatever happens on Friday, you've done us all proud.'

Chapter Ten

*H*I POLLY. THOUGHT *you should know a colleague of mine saw your text x*

Oops! Ever heard of password protection? X

Okay, my fault, I admit it x

Won't do it again and it was a joke. Wanted to see how you'd react x

Funny joke. Give me five minutes to recover x

Only took you two last time x

Stop it!

No kiss?

X

That's better. What you up to this weekend? X

Visiting my grandpa in Sussex x

Sussexy! If you change your mind, there's a hotel I know in Aberystwyth xx

Joking again or being polite? Xx

Neither. I lied. I really do need you inside me again xx

It's not going to happen xx

I'll tell Clara if you don't xx

She'll cross you off her Christmas card list if you do xx

God it's good to laugh. Not a lot of that down here xx

And so it goes on, which is fine by me, because it's better than sitting slumped on the sofa next to Doggo, watching a Jennifer Aniston romcom. I eventually ask Polly if it's okay to call her. It's great to hear her voice. I say I'm surprised Clara hasn't surfaced by now. I'm worried something bad might have happened to her.

'You don't have to be. Worried, I mean.' Clara has phoned home and spoken to their parents. It seems we were both wrong about Bali; she's in New Zealand. 'You mustn't say I told you.'

New Zealand rings a disturbing bell. Clara had a gig back in March styling a music video for a hot young Kiwi director who jetted in for a handful of high-profile jobs. Could that be what this is really about? She said she disliked the guy, but when I think back on it, she disliked him a touch too much. *He's so opinionated . . . so bloody sure of himself . . . so obsessed with details . . .* In short, all the things she likes in a man, all the things she used to like in me.

I'm an idiot. I should have read the signs. I feel suddenly sick. Who flies off to the other side of the world in the hope that a frisson might develop into something more? Not Clara, for sure; she's way too practical to roll the dice like that. No, she went knowing what lay in store for her, from which I can conclude – cue another brief surge of nausea – that she was having an affair with the guy right under my nose. (What was his name again? Wayne? I'll look it up later.)

I need to know the truth. I don't care what it takes. I'm as blind to the consequences as I was to the clues. The second I end my conversation with Polly, I call Clara's best friend, Fiona.

We've always got on well enough, although she falls into that category of 'friends' who I know will slowly fade from my life now that Clara is no longer a part of it. I've spoken to her a few times over the past couple of weeks, civil conversations. Something tells me this one isn't going to be.

After some opening pleasantries, I tell Fiona I'm thinking about calling in the police.

'The police?' There's a distinct note of alarm in her voice. 'I'm sure that's not necessary.'

'You reckon? For all I know, she's flown off to New Zealand to shag some director or other and he's beaten her to death and buried her body in the hills.'

The silence hangs between us like a wet blanket. 'Thanks for that, Dan.'

'Screw you, Fiona. I've been going half mad here.'

'She made me promise not to tell you.'

'Then screw her too.'

Childishly, I hang up before she can reply. Her text arrives a few minutes later: *She did what she needed to do. Maybe you should ask yourself why that is*

Jennifer Aniston sheds some tears on the TV while I tap away on my phone: *Here's the deal – I'll take your self-righteous crap if you tell me Will knows about Otto.* Will is her boyfriend, Otto an architect at the practice where she works. I want her to know that I'm in the loop about her brief fling; I want her to know that Clara is far from being the discreet and loyal friend she assumes her to be. There will definitely be consequences for their relationship. Cuckolded, cut adrift, I'm beyond caring. Let them slog it out. Here you are, the two of you, taste a little bit of the deceit, the pain, and see how it feels, because frankly, my dears, I don't give a damn.

I'll hate myself for it later, but right now it makes me feel a whole lot better about my roll in the hay with Polly. So much better, in fact, that I seriously consider calling her back and asking for the address of that hotel in Aberystwyth.

'Hey, Doggo, you want a weekend in Wales?'

He doesn't even glance at me; he's too intently focused on Jennifer, who's now looking gorgeously glum while dragging the back of her hand across her eyes to wipe away the tears.

I don't make the call to Polly. I can't blow Grandpa out, even though he has no idea I'm coming to visit him, even if, as happened last time, he struggles to place me in the fuzzy pantheon of family and friends who drop by the nursing home from time to time. The thing is, I love Grandpa, I always have, and his brain is going fast. I'll never forgive myself if the next chance I get to visit I find it's gone altogether.

The film ends, the credits roll, and Doggo does something he's never done before: he barks. I once heard him give a strangled sort of yelp when I accidentally trod on his paw in the kitchen, but this is the real thing, surprisingly deep and resonant given his size – like an apple-cheeked choirboy opening his mouth and belting out 'Ol' Man River' in a basso profundo.

'Doggo, shhhh.' But he doesn't let up, even when I find another movie to entertain him. He can't really have fallen that hard for Jennifer Aniston, can he? It's a frivolous thought, but as the racket continues, I figure it's got to be worth a shot. I pull up Film4+1, which runs exactly the same schedule an hour later. The moment we land back in the middle of the movie, Doggo falls silent and settles down, his big bug eyes glued to the screen, to Jennifer, who is hurrying along a pavement, yakking away to someone on her mobile.

I laugh and lay a tentative hand on Doggo's back. He's too distracted to protest.

'Good choice, you horny little devil.'

Chapter Eleven

RALPH IS IN raptures when the team returns to the office late on Friday afternoon. It seems Patrick outdid himself selling the concept to the suits at KP&G. Tristan was also present at the pitch and feels it went well.

'Compared to what?' asks Ralph, which sounds like a swipe at Tristan's lack of experience.

We won't have an answer until next week, but Ralph insists that the five of us – six including Doggo – decamp to the terrace bar at the Sanderson Hotel. He's keen to point out that we're not celebrating our success, just a job well done. 'No one can say we haven't given it our best shot. It's important to mark the small triumphs too.'

I understand his thinking; I'm made the same way. Edie and Tristan look less convinced. They'd prefer to know we had it in the bag before raising a glass. Patrick is just happy to bathe in the compliments (and, I suspect, the knowledge that his job is safe for the foreseeable future).

We down two bottles of champagne while Doggo laps at a bowl of water sweetly provided for him by our considerate waitress. I feel better than I have in a long while, surrounded by my new colleagues, my new life, the jolly banter. I even bum a cigarette off Edie. 'Smoking Kills. SWOSH! Doesn't,' chides Ralph. As ever, we all laugh along dutifully. Edie is the first to leave, followed closely by Tristan. When Patrick bids us both a good weekend and slips away, Ralph calls for the bill.

'Happy at Indology?' he asks me.

'Very.'

'I've got the feeling this is the start of something special – you and Edie, I mean.'

'Me too.'

'You don't have to agree with me just because I'm the boss.'

'Yes I do.'

He laughs. 'Tell me what you really think.'

'If I did that, you'd have to fire me.'

It's happening again, I'm morphing into Fat Trev, stealing his lines. It doesn't matter; he's not around to scream 'thief', and it's the kind of talk that goes down well with Ralph. I'm growing to really like the guy, not for his overbearing ebullience, but for the small things, such as suggesting the terrace bar at the Sanderson so that Doggo could come too rather than stay behind cooped up in the office; such as insisting on driving us home in his Bentley afterwards, despite it being a major detour for him.

I try to make Doggo sit at my feet, but he's having none of it. He clambers over me on to the back seat – just another leather sofa to stretch out on, as far as he's concerned.

'He's a funny little fellow,' observes Ralph. 'What's his story?'

I tell him what I know, which is next to nothing. I also tell him about Clara and her disappearing act, although I don't come clean about New Zealand and Wayne Kelsey. (I've looked him up, and from the lantern-jawed photos littering the Web, Wayne Kelsey could easily cast himself as the male lead in the debut feature film he's looking to get off the ground, 'a psychological thriller in the vein of Alfred Hitchcock's *Rebecca*'. Actually, not that you've probably ever read the book, you Kiwi fraud, it was Daphne du Maurier's *Rebecca*.)

Ralph reduces my circumstances to one word – 'Bummer' – before topping it off with some advice, a little trick he learned when his first wife left him for a young Dutchman. 'It's very simple. There's three things you have to say to yourself, over and over, like a mantra: She had her chance and she blew it . . . I'm not a bloody charity . . . She'll have to learn the hard way.' He slaps the steering wheel several times, crippled by his own humour.

We're nearing my flat when Ralph announces out of the blue, 'Don't take any shit from Tristan. If he starts throwing his weight around, just come to me.'

'Thanks, I will.'

'He's a smart guy, just not as smart as he thinks he is. Doesn't always know when to keep his mouth shut. Like this afternoon, kept sticking his bloody oar in, trying to run the show. Patrick did well not to lose his rhythm.'

Ah, so that explains the cruel dig at Tristan earlier.

Later, lying in the bath, it strikes me that Ralph was on a recruiting drive. A bit of tension at the top can be a healthy thing for any organisation, but I resolve to keep my head down, to stay out of whatever's brewing between the two alpha males. It's one of history's many valuable lessons: the foot soldiers tend to be the casualties in any conflict, not the generals.

★

It hardly warrants a tip-off to the pencil-pushers at Trades Descriptions, but you'd have to be perched high on one of its ugly brick chimney stacks for the Seaview Rest Home to stand any chance of living up to its name.

Maybe there was once a view of the sea, when the cumbersome Edwardian pile was first put up by some merchant or other on the rising ground to the north of Seaford. No longer. The town has spread, sprawling across the downland slopes like an ugly stain, and the house is now hedged in on all sides by other properties, reducing the view to a patch of sky.

You have to sign in and out, and beside the visitors' book in the entrance hall is a flip chart of daily quotations. Today's reads: MONEY ISN'T EVERYTHING, BUT IT SURE HELPS KEEP THE KIDS IN TOUCH. An old boy, bent by age, hovers nearby.

'They lie, you know? They all lie.'

'I'm sorry?'

'When they get here, when they leave.' He flashes me a set of perfect dentures. 'They're never here as long as they say.'

I glance at my watch and enter the time in the book: 11.32. He checks his watch, checks the book and seems satisfied, for now at least. 'We'll see,' he croaks mistrustfully.

The place is all swirly carpets, handrails, wheelchair ramps and eastern European carers on minimum wage. It has the distinct whiff about it of someone, somewhere, making a fast buck. It's hard to kill a cactus through neglect – they're hardy buggers – but the one on the windowsill in the corridor leading to my grandfather's ground-floor room is definitely on its last legs.

His room stinks of stale piss, which is upsetting and

unacceptable. Even if he's had a mishap, forty thousand pounds a year (or is it fifty?) should buy a thorough cleaning job. Let's face it, all they have to do for their money is feed him terrible food three times a day, wipe his ass every so often and bath him twice a week. The rest of the time he spends in his armchair, dozing or staring blankly at the blue-and-white-striped wallpaper (hats off to the decorators for their bars-of-a-cage theming).

There are a lot of grim diseases around, but Alzheimer's is right up there with the worst of them. They call it 'the long goodbye' and I can see why. Over the past couple of years I've watched Grandpa's mind wither away. The steady stream of anecdotes for which he was known has all but dried up, and only if you're lucky will you catch a flash of his wicked sense of humour. I did the last time I visited, when a cute young carer poked her head into his room to check if everything was okay.

'Ah, Magda. Can't stay away. Any excuse to drop by. She says it's my body she's after, but I know it's my money.'

'Very funny, Mr Larssen.'

'I've told her I'm married, but does she listen?'

These momentary flarings of his old self are becoming increasingly rare. Soon they will stop altogether. He'll be reduced to a husk, a series of bodily functions and little else.

He looks so peaceful in his armchair, head back, eyes closed, that I decide to leave him be. I perch on his bed and observe him. Even at the age of eighty-two, there's nothing frail or shrunken about him. He's a solid block of a man, tall, broad, impressive. The jagged scar on his left hand looks strangely livid today. I know the story behind it, even if he can no longer recall it. It's a souvenir of the German bombing of Coventry on the night of 14 November 1940. He was seven years old at the time, the eldest child of first-generation Danish immigrants. He lost his best friend in the explosion that vaporised the neighbours' house and brought the best part of their own crashing down on their heads (and his hand).

As a young boy I listened in rapt horror to his tales of that night, of the terrible things he witnessed. They're my stories now; they're no longer his to tell. Maybe I'll pass them on to my own children, but just how long they survive before they fade forever into nothingness is anybody's guess.

He opens his eyes, smiles weakly. 'Oh, it's you.'

'Hi, Grandpa. How are you doing?'

He stirs, stretches out his long legs. 'The strangest thing happened the other day.'

'Oh?'

'A small volcano appeared, just here . . .' He gingerly lays a hand on his left knee. 'It gave off two tiny puffs of smoke – pfff, pfff – then it disappeared.'

I'm struggling to keep a straight face. 'Wow.'

He frowns at me. 'It's amazing, Annie, you look just like Daniel today.'

Annie is my mother, his daughter. 'It's me, Grandpa – Daniel.'

'How is he?'

'Grandpa, it's me, Daniel. I'm fine.'

'Have you heard from him?'

I give up and go with it. 'Yes, he's got a new job.'

'A new job. That's good. Good boy. Has he married that girl yet?'

79

'Clara?'

'The one with the long hair. The one you don't like.'

Well, that's news.

'No, not yet,' I reply.

'And his book? Has he finished it?'

Finished? Try started. 'It's getting there,' I lie.

'I can't wait to read it. I like a good book, and I know it'll be a good book.'

It's a beautiful day, so I suggest a drive – to Alfriston maybe, or Birling Gap, places he often took me to when I was a youngster. The names no longer seem to mean anything to him. 'Birling Gap? I don't think so, Annie. Not today. I'm very tired.'

He closes his eyes and drifts off again. I wonder if they've got him on something. This thought is enough to drive me to my feet and down the corridor, where the head sister (who clearly doesn't appreciate my tone) assures me that he's not drugged up to the eyeballs; it's just that he's not sleeping well at night and therefore dozing more during the day to make up for it. Expecting to scoop Grandpa up and bolt, I've left Doggo in the car. I now go and grab him. He's sitting in the passenger seat, sulking at being abandoned. I know the look – a heavy-lidded sidelong glance – and I've learned that mimicking it is the best way to defuse his mood. It's still a good minute before he finally cracks and follows me inside.

Doggo seems taken with the sight of Grandpa slumbering in his armchair. He pricks up his ears, turns to look at me and then does something completely unexpected: he hops up on to Grandpa's lap.

Grandpa stirs. 'Hello, you. What's your name?'

'Doggo,' I say.

'Doggo, eh? God, you're an ugly little bugger. Yes you are . . . yes you are . . .' Doggo doesn't seem to mind having his ears fiddled with and his snout scratched.

Grandpa looks up at me suddenly. 'You haven't told him, have you?'

'Who? Doggo?'

'Don't be ridiculous. Daniel, of course.'

'Told him what?'

His eyes narrow mistrustfully. 'You have, haven't you?'

He looks so distressed that I find myself saying, 'No, no, of course I haven't.'

'Thank God,' he says, visibly relaxing. 'One father is enough for any man.'

I don't expect to get through to her, and because I'm phoning Spain on my mobile, I'm not too unhappy when it goes straight to message.

'Mum, it's me, Daniel. Give me a call when you've got a chance.'

I've let Doggo off his lead and he's zigzagging along beside me, happy as Larry, sniffing out God knows what in the long grass trimming the pathway beside the river.

This may well be my favourite place on the planet: Cuckmere Haven, where the Cuckmere river meets the English Channel. It's an affection bound up with all kinds of childhood memories. We used to come here and drop into the river and be swept out to sea, where ridged sandbanks would magically rise up beneath our eager feet, allowing us to stand and stare back at the pebbled shoreline and the blinding white chalk cliffs flanking the low river valley.

The geography is just the same, but the trimmings have changed. The pathways are now of compacted gravel designed to take a wheelchair (nothing wrong with that), there are rubbish bins every hundred yards or so (when once we all knew to lug our litter back to the car), and the place is bristling with signs. There are signs pointing out the oxbow lake where the meandering river has cut a corner at the end of its journey, others indicating exactly how far it is to Seaford or Eastbourne by foot along the coastal path, yet more listing the local flora and fauna. Worst of all, there are signs in red beside the river that read: DANGER! NO SWIMMING. There's even some small print recording the local by-law you'll be infringing if you dare to ignore the warning.

We were made to feel like spineless little cowards if we didn't hurl ourselves into the Cuckmere and brave the clash of fresh and salt water. Nowadays, there are laws forbidding it. Has the world really changed that much in my brief lifetime? Evidently, and that realisation saddens me.

To the east of the beach lie the Seven Sisters, the oscillating stretch of chalk cliffs that film-makers have always used to stand in for the white cliffs of Dover because they're so much more photogenic than the real thing. Doggo and I are now standing at the exact spot where Kevin Costner, in the role of Robin Hood (complete with cape, dodgy mullet and American accent), once prostrated himself on returning from the Crusades in a rowboat.

I re-enact it for Doggo's benefit, rolling around laughing and proclaiming loudly, 'I'm home! I'm home!' Doggo looks on with the same mix of scorn and bewilderment that Morgan Freeman brought to the character of Robin's Saracen buddy.

We're heading back to the car when the urge suddenly takes me, fired by those words stamped in red capitals: DANGER! NO SWIMMING. I strip off down to my boxer shorts, and leaving no time for common sense to take hold, I leap into the river. Christ, it's cold. It's also swollen and fast-flowing after the recent rains. Doggo bounds along, keeping pace with me as the fierce current carries me off. He draws to a sudden halt, his whole body twitching in anticipation, then he launches himself off the high bank and belly-flops into the water. He seems to be smiling as he paddles furiously to draw alongside me.

'Do you come here often?' I ask.

He barks twice. It sounds remarkably like 'Fuck off.'

The best bit is when the river gives way to the sea and the water suddenly corrugates. You switchback through the crests and troughs, rising and falling, the force of the current at your back gradually diminishing until you can finally affect the course of your trajectory. The sandbanks are still there, and the sensation of the gloopy sand mingled with river mud oozing between my toes carries me back twenty years. I reach for Doggo and draw him to me. It's the first time I've ever held him in my arms. Amazingly, he doesn't growl.

We're making our way back up the path to my abandoned clothes when I spot the man hurrying towards us. His green uniform suggests he's an official of some kind.

'Can't you read? It says no swimming.' Puce with indignation, he stabs his finger at one of the signs.

'I wasn't swimming, I was rescuing my dog.'

That throws him, but not for long. 'I don't believe you,' he blusters.

'It's true, he just jumped in.' I turn to Doggo. 'Doggo! Bad Doggo!'

It's the wrong thing to say, because they're the exact words I used in reprimand when he bit Megan, and on that occasion he was rewarded with a Choc Drop. Maybe anticipating the same, he promptly leaps back into the river.

I give the man a shrug, then jump in after him.

It's even more fun the second time.

'Ems, it's me.'

'Hey, Dan.'

'Bad time?'

'Only if you're driving.'

'Don't worry, I've got you on speaker.'

'Hang up. I'm not going to collude in a criminal act.'

'What the hell, Ems?'

'Just pull over and call me back.'

My mother has been with Nigel for fifteen years, most of which they've spent in Spain, living a life of luxury in a sprawling old farmhouse in the hills behind Malaga. Nigel is very wealthy, wealthy enough to foot the bill for Grandpa's nursing home without even blinking. The talk has always been of a hefty inheritance from a bachelor uncle, but this has done nothing to dampen my suspicions that the antiques business Nigel used to own in Arundel was a front for some far more nefarious business activity. It wouldn't surprise me. For all his many charms, there's something essentially shifty about him.

They rarely return to England, and when they do, the two

of them are pretty insufferable, flaunting their leathery perma-tans and distributing bottles of virgin olive oil pressed from the fruit of their own trees. Emma has always been much better at staying in touch with them than I have.

'I think they might be in Morocco.'

I'm now standing in a lay-by near Lewes. 'Morocco?'

'They're thinking of building a house near Essaouira.'

'Why would they want to do that?'

'Er, because they want to, because they can.'

'Lucky them.'

'Lucky us, too, if they decide to go ahead. When you speak to Mum, be enthusiastic. Come to think of it, don't bother, she'll know you're putting it on. Anyway, why are you suddenly so keen to talk to her?'

'It was something Grandpa said.'

'What?'

I want to tell her, and I almost do, but the implications are way too big for both of us. 'It's probably nothing.'

'Facebook her if it's urgent.'

'Facebook? Mum?'

'Only for three years. And it's time you signed up, luddite. How is he?'

'Grandpa? Oh, you know, not getting any better. You should come and see him before it's too late.'

An articulated lorry thunders by, drowning out Emma's reply. 'Sorry, I missed that.'

'I said it's easier for you, you don't have a family . . . kids.'

I know my sister. Telling her it's a poor excuse is the wrong way to come at the thing. 'You're right. Don't bother. It doesn't matter.'

'No, no, I must, I will, I want to.'

'Don't leave it too long. If the volcano that appeared on his knee the other day really blows its top, you might not get another chance.'

'You're joking.'

'I wish.'

'A volcano? That's priceless.'

It's good to hear her laugh. It's been a while.

Chapter Twelve

WE'VE WON THE SWOSH! account!

Doggo is watching episode three of the first season of *Friends* and Edie and I are playing pool against Clive and Connor when Ralph tips up with Tristan to deliver the news. They're ecstatic. We're ecstatic. Everyone's ecstatic. The creative department soon fills with well-wishers. Champagne appears from somewhere. Doggo weaves through the forest of legs wondering what he's done to bring about such a merry gathering in his honour. His self-delusion is more understandable since word ripped through the office about his bizarre obsession with Jennifer Aniston. For the past couple of days people have been dropping by to see for themselves. He's had heaps of attention, and he's getting more of it now. Margaret in Accounts is still miffed that she can't bring her cat to work, but she's the one who says to Doggo: 'Well, well, well, you're turning out to be a proper little mascot, aren't you?'

It's even better than we expected. Ralph was right: KP&G fell hard for the idea at the pitch last Friday; they just wanted some time to run the concept past the marketing consultancy they use. 'There's a guy there, Ben Wood, a bloody genius if ever I met one. He's convinced the concept can travel, go international.' This is huge news. It'll give Indology a foreign profile, opening up lucrative new markets for future business.

I catch Edie's eye across the crowded room and wonder if she's thinking the same thing as I am: that we really are a team now, a genuine partnership, not just two people beavering away in a back office, hoping for the best. Fat Trev pops into my head. I've been a coward; I really need to get my skates on. If he doesn't already know about my new job at Indology, he will soon enough. Tristan will no doubt use all his clout with *Campaign* to ensure that news of the SWOSH! account receives the biggest possible splash at the magazine.

Ralph calls for silence, then pays a touching tribute to Tristan for his instinct about pairing Edie and me. Tristan promptly blows the moment, taking the floor and holding forth on how SWOSH! 'synchromeshes' with his vision of where Indology is headed. Intended as a motivational team talk, it comes across as a dull homily. I can feel the energy draining from the room. It only returns when Ralph announces on a sudden whim that we can all take the rest of the day off. 'What the hell,' he chortles. 'Just make sure you spend it unwisely.'

Tristan isn't the sort of boss to indulge the workers, and I glance at him expecting to read disapproval in his face. What I see is the fleeting look he exchanges with Edie before she quickly averts her gaze. Maybe I'm wrong, but I could swear there was something complicit, even illicit, in the momentary meeting of their eyes.

Putting it to the test is easy enough. Edie isn't up for frittering away the afternoon with me in celebration. 'I'd love to, but I've got a ton of stuff to catch up on,' she offers feebly. Then, as everyone is dispersing, I collar Tristan and suggest lunch – just him and me, my treat, by way of a thank you. 'You don't have to thank me for making me look good,' he jokes. He claims to have some shopping he urgently needs to do, and the free afternoon is a rare opportunity to pick up his young son from school. I have a strong suspicion he won't be standing at the school gates later.

Did I misread the look that passed between them? It's quite possible. I've spent the last few days in a deeply suspicious frame of mind, ever since Grandpa dropped his bombshell at the nursing home: *One father is enough for any man.*

His words have had me picking at the past like it's a scabby knee, wondering what lies I've been peddled over the years. Admittedly, Grandpa thought he was talking to my mother at the time, so he can hardly be described as being of sound mind, but my gut tells me he spoke that line from some clean, untouched corner of his diseased brain (which then shut down completely the moment I pressed him to elaborate).

I've tried to construe what he said in any number of ways, but only one interpretation holds water: that the man I have always thought of as my father may well not be my real father. It seems ridiculous, but it's not inconceivable. People have always remarked that I take after my mother in the looks department. The mouths are strong and the noses long on her side of the family. The Larssens are also tall, which I suppose I am, and which my father definitely isn't. I shot past him when I was fourteen years old, the year before he and Mum divorced. Could there be a correlation? Did he look up at me and think, 'That lanky monster can't possibly be mine'? Did he confront Mum? Did she confess under duress? It's possible. Then again, anything's possible once you're trapped in the paranoid world I've been inhabiting since Saturday.

Emma and I have always been led to believe that Dad fell in love with a colleague, a fellow lecturer in modern history at the University of East Anglia. I remember Mum telling us at the time, 'Your father has left me for a lesbian. Somehow, I think I'll get over it,' which gives some idea of what my mother is like: not great when it comes to delicacy of touch in situations requiring it.

I'm not convinced Carol is a lesbian, although I suppose she might once have been one. She's a bit younger than Dad, which means she went through university in the mid 1970s, when being straight probably marked you out as someone who condoned the massacre of innocent Vietnamese freedom fighters. I'm being facetious, of course, but only because it's easy to be when it comes to Carol, to the two of them, in fact. When the Berlin Wall fell in 1989, it took most of their left-leaning theories with it. I was only seven at the time, but I remember Dad's blank stare as we watched the East Berliners on TV taking their sledgehammers to that symbolic wall, reducing it to rubble.

Dad proved to be more resilient, twisting his arguments to fit the new, post-communist age. To admit he'd been wrong all along would have been career suicide. Switching horses in midstream doesn't go down well in academia. It's like those art historians who built their reputations on theories about the sombre colours of the ceiling frescoes in the Sistine Chapel bearing witness to Michelangelo's depressive state of mind at the time, only for the true, almost garish vibrancy of the master's palette to be revealed when centuries of grime were finally removed. Did those professors hold up their hands and admit it was a fair cop? No, they went on the attack, falling over each other to discredit the cleaning process that had also stripped away their academic standing.

Dad has always been a remote man, caught up in his studies and his writing, his mind on higher things, but it strikes me now that, if anything, he grew even more withdrawn following the divorce, whereas most men would surely have extended themselves with their children to take the sting out of the separation. Emma is hardly ever present when I see him, so I can't say for sure whether he's different with her, more loving, more 'fatherly'.

I followed Emma's advice and did something I swore I'd never do: sign up to Facebook. Mum accepted me as a 'friend' and then promptly made me do something else I swore I'd never do: sign up to Skype.

We've set a time to talk. I can't believe it'll work, but it does. At exactly 8 p.m. she appears as if by magic on my laptop screen in a white halter-top blouse, or possibly a dress (I can't say for sure because she's seated at a table). Behind her is a swimming pool fringed with palm trees. The sun has yet to set in Morocco and there's a glass of white wine in her hand.

'Danny,' she beams.

She's the only person I allow to call me that. 'Hi, Mum. How are things?'

'Oh, you know – coping,' she jokes, with a nod over her shoulder.

We haven't communicated in months, so I tell her about the

new job and the account that Edie and I have just won for the agency.

'Mouthwash? That's great!'

I know she's happy for me; she doesn't mean it to sound like an insult. And it's not as if I make it easy for her. My biggest successes to date have included oven chips ('That's wonderful, darling. What are oven chips?') and fabric softener ('I'll switch brands immediately').

'Mum, there's something I need to talk to you about. Are you alone?'

'Alone? Yes.'

Not convincing.

'Good,' I say, 'because it's about Nigel. Maria called me in a state. She's carrying his child and she doesn't know what to do.' Maria is the dark beauty who cooks, cleans, shops and generally runs their lives for them.

Nigel's face appears at the side of the screen. 'Lies, damned lies. The paternity test will prove it.' You have to hand it to him, he's funny and quick on his feet. 'Looking good, Daniel.'

'You too, Nigel,' I reply, although I'm not convinced by the collarless shirt and paisley cravat combo.

'If you want a word in private with the old bag, that's fine by me — I'm gone.' He waggles his fingers, then disappears from the screen.

'Old bag?' Mum calls after him.

'Vintage,' I hear Nigel say out of shot.

Naturally, being her son, I'm slightly repulsed by the look of love in her eyes, but I'm also moved by it. The truth is, she married a curmudgeon the first time around and has been given a second shot at happiness. There's a danger that I'm about to shake up her life in ways she doesn't want, need or deserve, but I have to have it out with her.

She listens in silence to the account of my visit to the Seaview Rest Home, but when I tell her what Grandpa said to me, thinking I was her, she gives a loud and amused snort. 'He said that?'

'He did. In all seriousness.'

She stares straight at me and says, as if speaking to the village idiot, 'Danny, Grandpa is off with the fairies.'

I want to ask her how she knows that, seeing as she hasn't set eyes on him since Christmas. 'Not completely. Not yet.'

'Come on, it's rubbish, nonsense.'

'Is it, Mum? Is it really? I have to ask. You must see that.'

'I do. I understand. But you're not thinking straight and we both know why.'

'Meaning?'

'I heard what happened with Clara.'

'Oh?'

'Emma told me.'

'And you didn't think to call me?'

'And *you* didn't think to call *me*?' she fires back. 'No, you didn't, because we don't have that kind of relationship any more. Thank God. You're a man now, thirty years old, for goodness' sake. You really want your mother meddling in your affairs? I have great belief in you, Danny. You'll sort out whatever needs to be sorted out. You've always been like that – strong, independent, wilful. Oh yes, certainly wilful.'

I've played this conversation over and over in my mind. I've imagined what she would say and what I would say in return. I now reach for one of those rehearsed lines.

'Mum, listen, nobody else needs to know, not Emma, not Nigel, not even Dad if he doesn't already. But I do. It's my right, you know it is.'

'What I *know*,' she corrects me, hardening, 'is that you're working yourself into a state over nothing. At best, at worst, it's wishful thinking on Grandpa's part. He was never a fan of your father. I'm sorry to have to say it, but it's true.'

I know it's true because she has hammered home the point over the years, as she well knows.

'Swear it on Grandpa's life.'

'What?'

'You heard. Swear on the life of your own father that Dad is my biological father.'

I watch her take a sip of wine. 'What a horrid thing to ask. But if it makes you feel better, I do – I swear. There. Are you happy now?'

Yes. And also disgusted with myself. 'I'm sorry, Mum.'

'So am I. But it's not your fault, or Grandpa's, it's the Alzheimer's. Just try and be a bit more, well, circumspect about what comes out of his mouth.'

'I will.'

'Now show me this new dog of yours Emma mentioned.'

Doggo and I definitely had a bonding moment in the Cuckmere river – I've had stroking and ear-fiddling rights conceded to me since then – but I know that if I call him he won't come, so I unplug my laptop and carry it to the sofa.

'Gosh,' says my mother. 'He's hardly a shoo-in for Crufts, is he?'

Chapter Thirteen

Only when I wake do I realise just how much the Grandpa thing had been dragging me down. I feel light, liberated, at peace with the world.

Clara used to kick off the day with a few minutes of silent contemplation, a sort of private prayer, offering thanks for the precious gift of life and resolving to honour it through her actions. I tried it for a while, the two of us seated in the lotus position on the living room floor, facing each other. Then one morning she told me to breathe through my anus. I was never able to keep a straight face after that, and soon found myself banned from the morning ritual.

On my own, it works a whole lot better, even with the distraction of Doggo circling me, curious but aloof. I let the important realities of my situation seep into me: I'm healthy, young(ish), gainfully employed and living in a country that cherishes personal freedoms. This makes me considerably better off than billions of other people on the planet. Any miseries in my life are either unavoidable or of my own making.

No stranger has stepped from the shadows and killed someone I love in a random act of violence. Yes, a month ago my girlfriend ran off to be with another man, but the truth is, I'd grown lazy, not just with Clara, with myself too. I spent six months in a self-indulgent slump following Fat Trev's breakdown, wallowing in my misfortune. It was the opportunity I'd been waiting for to finally launch into the novel. Lack of time was no longer an excuse, so I dredged up some others. Clara could easily have flung them back in my face, but she waited patiently for inspiration to strike and my fingers to start dancing across the keyboard.

I should have known she'd lose faith in me before too long; she's always searching for something new, or somebody new, to believe in. Well, she found Kamael, her guardian angel, and then she latched on to Wayne Kelsey. I hope they're happy together, all three of them, I really do. I am, it occurs to me, finally coming to terms with the fact that our relationship is well and truly over.

It's fine. No one died. Everyone's alive and well. Okay, not Grandpa – he's alive and rather poorly – but even his slow decline has to be accepted as one of those things that life throws at us. Mum was wrong: Alzheimer's isn't to blame. How can you blame something that acts with no malice, which is simply buried away in the genetic code of a person like a ticking bomb?

And does it really matter whether Grandpa spoke the truth or not, whether or not Mum lied to me from her poolside perch in Morocco last night? I'm alive. It's enough. It's more than enough. No, it's a miracle. Not in any religious sense of the word. I lost my faith a good while back. I mean, the major religions can't all be right, and given that they're so manifestly wrong about where we've come from, I'm not sure we should take too seriously anything they have to say about where we're going. I'm pretty sure, however, that I don't want to spend all of eternity in a place inherited by the meek.

Feeling myself drifting off message, I take a few deep breaths, exhaling slowly through pursed lips.

Edie, I think. Ah, Edie – smart, fun, beautiful Edie. So what if she's having an affair with Tristan? Who am I to judge her, them? Maybe he's married to an awful woman who demeans him the moment he crosses the threshold at the end of every day, who berates him for being a bad father, who maliciously chips away at his sense of self-worth. And what of Edie's boyfriend, Douglas? I know he's a sports nut who plays rugby all winter then switches seamlessly to cricket for the summer months. He trains two evenings a week and is often away at weekends. Who wouldn't feel neglected, unappreciated, ignored?

Maybe Tristan is destined to find true happiness with Edie the second time around, as my mother did with Nigel. I'm certainly not entitled to set myself up as some kind of moral authority, not after leaping into bed with the sister of my only-just-ex-girlfriend.

Satisfied with the place my mini meditation has transported me to, I open my eyes to find Doggo now sitting right in front of me. I reach out a hand and stroke him. He tilts his head so that his ears also get a good going-over.

'I'm sorry, Doggo, I haven't been myself.' Something in his big liquid eyes suggests that I'm not telling him anything he doesn't already know. 'I'll make it up to you, I promise.'

Our morning routine is for me to grab a double macchiato from the Portuguese café up the road, which I sip en route to Athlone Gardens, where Doggo sniffs around a bit before taking his morning dump. We then double back to Ladbroke Grove, where I ditch my coffee cup and his bagged shit in the litter bin beside the bus stop. We've honed our timing to perfection; we rarely have to wait more than two minutes for the bus.

The voice, which I ignore at first, comes from the block of council flats that doesn't so much front Athlone Gardens as occupy a chunk of it.

'Oi, you with the dog. Yeah, you. What's your game?'

A large man with a shaven head is peering down at me from a second-floor balcony. Still in his pyjamas, he's smoking a cigarette.

'Excuse me?'

'You live here?' he asks.

'No.'

'Quasimodo?'

'Sorry?'

'The dog, you doughnut.'

'Er, no, he doesn't.'

'So what makes you think you can bring it here to shit?'

I'm about to reply, quite reasonably, that it's a public park, but I don't get a chance to.

'You want me to come round your place and have my dog shit on your doorstep?'

'I always bag it.'

'Yeah? So will I. Twice a day. Just like you.'

'I'm sorry.'

'Wot?'

'I'm sorry. If it upsets you, I'll stop.'

'Wot?'

He's obviously itching for an argument, but I'm damned if I'm going to let him haul me down off my karmic cloud. Clara comes to my aid in the form of one of her favourite phrases. I raise my hand high and call, 'Love and light.'

The man falls strangely still, then his hand slowly rises to return the gesture. It's a beautiful moment . . . until the hand swivels, the fingers folding back so that only the middle one remains, perfectly upright.

'I got my eye on you, weirdo.'

The story draws a smile from Edie, but not much more.

She has been a bit subdued all week, and I think I know the reason why. The aftermath is always tough for us creatives. The moment the account is won, our job is effectively done. We may have landed the fish, but it's for others to gut it, fillet it and cook it. At best, our opinion will be sought from time to time by planning, design and production, but it's poor consolation after the buzz of victory, which fades all too fast.

I've been in a bit of a funk too, and we've been shooting a lot of pool. It's the glue that binds the creative department together. Colleagues cum rivals, we play as we work, in a spirit of good-natured competitiveness. Megan and Seth are currently top of the box league, followed by Eric and Josh from design (whose graphics skills have earned them honorary membership of the creative club), then Clive and Connor, with Edie and me in the bottom spot. New to the game, Edie is still infuriated that she's holding us back. She won't be for long, not at the rate she's practising in her lunch hours. She also confessed to me the other day that she's found a pub with a pool table near her flat so she can hone her game away from work with Douglas.

It's a determination that verges on obsession, and it lays her open to Megan's mockery. Megan excels at mockery. She dresses it up as playful joshing, but you can't help feeling there's a splinter of genuine hostility buried away in there somewhere. It's the same with her smile, which is big and freely given but also mildly unsettling, because her eyes never quite seem to be smiling too. I'm pretty sure she hates having us around and isn't going to change her mind any time soon. We haven't set out to challenge her hold over her ragtag posse of slightly hopeless young men, but our refusal to play along with her mother-hen antics inevitably calls her authority into question. I'm guessing that's how she sees it.

If I'm aware of Seth perking up every time he finds himself in Edie's presence, then so is Megan. She's a watcher. I'm coming round to Seth, partly out of pity that he gets to sit in an office all day with Megan, but mainly because he's sweet with Doggo, chatting away to him like he's a human being: 'Doggo, you'll never guess what, the weirdest thing happened to me at the weekend . . .' I have a sneaking suspicion it's his way of letting Edie know a bit more about who he is, what makes him tick. 'Hey, Doggo, I was at the Gaga concert at the O2 last night with a bunch of friends . . .'

Clive and Connor, I've decided, are a couple of bona fide oddballs, best avoided, which isn't hard. They like to keep themselves to themselves, their door closed, the music loud (to drown out the sound of their constant bickering). They're like a couple of foul-mouthed old fishwives, even when they're playing pool.

'Not that one. I put it there to cover the pocket.'

'You were trying to pot it and missed, you English twat!'

'Even if you're right, which you aren't, because you're a thick-as-shite bog-Irish eejit, it's still the wrong bloody shot.'

Et cetera. Ad nauseam. Patrick's theory is that they're in love with each other but haven't got round to admitting they're gay. Then again, it took Patrick almost thirty years to admit it to himself, so the notion of repressed homosexuality maybe figures larger in his thinking than it should.

Patrick has come to life since he clinched the SWOSH! account for the agency, and has been showering us with gifts as well as gratitude. Edie and I both went home the other night with bottles of vintage Dom Perignon champagne, Doggo with a silver disc (engraved with his name and my mobile number) dangling from a brand-new leather collar. The name tag has settled the debate – Doggo is Doggo – although I don't suppose he was ever really going to be anything else.

I look for him now but he's not on his sofa. Odds are he's with Anna, the sweet young thing who replaced Edie on reception. She spoils him something rotten.

An email lands in my inbox. I glance at my laptop and freeze. It's from Clara. My mind swiftly makes the calculation (as it has many times before): just after 9 p.m. in New Zealand. I check my watch: twenty minutes to go before our meeting with Tristan. Maybe I should wait until afterwards. But what if she isn't there later? I open the email.

I'm ready to talk now x

I stare at the words. Is that really all she can offer after everything she's put me through? Is it a joke? Five words and one kiss? I know I should sit on it for a few minutes, allow myself to calm down, but my fingers take on a life of their own.

That's great! I'm close too. Just give me another decade.

I glance over at Edie while I'm waiting for the reply. She catches my look. 'What?'

'Nothing,' I reply.

PING.

You're hurting and I understand.

I wasn't before, but I am now. An unwelcome image blows into my mind: Clara sitting in the living room of Wayne Kelsey's no doubt ridiculously hip pad, loved up, glass of Sauvignon Blanc at her elbow, tapping away, closing a chapter in her life with a few lazy words. Not even one whiff of apology.

If an overwhelming sense of relief that I don't have to deal with your narcissistic New Age bullshit ever again counts as hurting, then yes, I'm suffering all the torments of hell.

Hardly in the live-and-let-live spirit of this morning's meditation, it occurs to me.

This only confirms I did the right thing.

Funny, that. When have you ever done the wrong thing?

I wait for her reply. When it doesn't arrive, I start composing another email.

'Come on, what's up?'

I look across at Edie. 'Nothing.'

'You're grunting.'

'I'm not grunting. I don't grunt.'

'And you'll break your keyboard if you keep typing like that.'

I come clean, show her the exchange. She reads it over my shoulder, her hands on the back of my chair. 'Ouch,' she says at one point, and when she's done: 'Well, I'm not hearing wedding bells.'

'My fault? Her fault?'

'Does it matter?' When I don't reply, she says, 'You were tough, but she was cold as clay.'

'There speaks the daughter of a potter.'

Edie smiles, wanders back to her desk. 'She wants to meet you.'

'Who?'

'The potter.'

'Really?'

'Yeah, beats me too.'

That's when Doggo scampers into the room with a letter in his mouth. He has grown much more intrepid recently, roaming freely about the place, and I assume at first that he's nabbed the letter off someone's desk. But Anna comes hurrying in behind him.

'He did it! All I said was "Take this to Dan."'

I'm surprised and touched. 'He knows my name.'

'He knows where the Choc Drops are,' mutters Edie.

'No, he knows my name too. Test him.' Anna drifts off towards the sofa, and when I ask, 'Where's Anna?' Doggo turns his head and looks at her.

'You see! He's super-smart.'

'He's been hiding his light under a bushel.' Doggo still has the letter in his mouth. I swap it for a Choc Drop and wrestle him to the ground. 'Who's a brainy boy? Yes you are, my little Einstein.'

We roll around, him growling his I'm-only-just-okay-with-this growl.

★

Ralph's kids are on half-term this week and he has flown off to Mallorca with them, leaving Tristan to hold the fort. For an intelligent guy, Tristan seems to have very little sense of his impact on others. Can't he hear the mutterings in the ranks? He has expanded to fill the space vacated by Ralph with a touch too much eagerness for some people. There's a new swagger about him, topped off with a dose of ingratiating smarm.

In a parody of self-importance, he even has his heels on his desk when Edie and I join him in his office. He's perusing a file.

'No rest for the wicked. This just came in.'

He skims the file across the desk towards us. It's a brief for a longer-lasting hair colourant.

'"Dye Another Day",' I toss out, joking.

'That's good,' says Tristan. 'Damn, that's good!'

Which only goes to show how little he really knows about the business. First off, 'dye' has long been out of favour when it comes to hair, too harsh and chemical in its connotations. You dye clothes; you colour hair. Secondly, what client would want to associate their product with one of the worst ever Bond films?

When I mention this, Tristan looks affronted. 'It's my favourite Bond.'

'Seriously?'

It can't be. It's got Madonna in it, not to mention the most absurd twist of all time, when beautiful fine-boned Toby Stephens turns out to be the genetically remastered North Korean nemesis from the opening sequence.

'Actually, no,' says Tristan. '*Licence to Kill.*'

That's even lower down my list than *Die Another Day*, which at least had Bond doing what Bond does best – saving the world from another high-functioning psychopath. In *Licence to Kill*, Timothy Dalton goes rogue, running all over Florida to exact revenge on a Latin American drug lord.

'It's like a bad Stallone movie but with a bigger budget.'

Edie comes to Tristan's defence. 'It's got a great opening sequence.'

She's right, it does. She clearly knows her Bond films.

'What's your favourite?' I ask her.

I figure she'll go for Connery – *Goldfinger*, maybe, or *From Russia with Love*.

'*Casino Royale*.'

Good choice. Daniel Craig's first outing as 007, and still his best. Edie and I are quoting lines from the train scene at each other, the one where Bond first meets Vesper Lynd, when Tristan irritably draws the discussion to a close and dismisses us. 'Actually, Dan, a quick word.'

He wants to talk about the lunch I proposed last week, the one he couldn't make because he was probably shagging Edie in some squalid little hotel in Victoria (I'm more convinced of it than ever after observing them together just now). We set a date for next Tuesday, but he's not done with me yet. He wants some advice. I've heard from Edie that he's writing a business book on the side; she didn't tell me it was going to 'turn accepted management practices on their head'. I'm even more intrigued when he says it's inspired by the teachings of Montaigne.

'Montaigne?'

'The French philosopher.'

I know who Montaigne is. I was made to read his *Essais* at university, and very good they were too. However, I'm pretty sure he didn't have a whole lot to say about capitalist command structures, if only because he lived in the pre-capitalist sixteenth century. Apparently that doesn't matter.

'With a book like this you need a hook, a USP, and I've gone with Montaigne.'

'Why?'

'Because he was a sceptic, and a lot of my theories are very . . .' He searches for the word.

'Sceptical?' I suggest.

'Now, now,' he says. 'No need to be facetious.'

'Theories' is something of an exaggeration. As far as I can tell, he only has one: that a surfeit of managers generates inertia, slowing the system down, because to question and impede is the natural tendency of a person who's out to keep their place in an organisation. 'I mean, if you said yes to everything that crossed your desk, what's the point of you even being there? They might as well fire you and save themselves a salary.'

It's an interesting proposition, even if it does sound suspiciously like Parkinson's law. It also rides on the back of a massive assumption: that all ideas are good and should be allowed to travel unimpeded to the top. I'm guessing that layers of management are pretty effective at wheedling out the sort of crap ideas that could bring a business to its knees. I don't say anything to Tristan. No doubt he has marshalled his arguments and cherry-picked a bunch of case studies to bear out his hypothesis.

'De-Management or Anti-Management?' he asks.

'Sorry?'

'For the title.'

I think on it for a moment. 'Anti is too strident. De-Management suggests a positive process . . . cutting out the dead wood.'

His smile suggests that I've just confirmed his own instinct. 'I'm going to need a tag-line for the cover. It's a must with books like this: *De-Management: How to blah blah blah* . . . you know the sort of thing.'

I sure do: *How to Make a Fortune Flogging a Specious Management Theory to Gullible Businessmen*. I'm happy to help out – well, not really, but I can't exactly say no.

'Maybe I should read a bit of it to get a better idea of what you're up to.'

He hands me the chapter he's just finished. It's headed 'If You're Not at the Table, You're on the Menu'. To his credit, it actually sounds like something Montaigne might have said.

Chapter Fourteen

THE INVITATION FROM Edie comes late on Thursday as I'm leaving work to go and meet Fat Trev. (I haven't told her I'm seeing him because I sense she's threatened by him, possibly even worried we'll rekindle our partnership once he's back on an even keel.)

She has a wedding at the weekend out near Henley, someone she knew when she was growing up, and Douglas is off in Shropshire playing cricket. 'I know it's short notice, and you're probably doing something already.'

'You want me to be your plus one?'

'Plus two, although Doggo might have to skip the wedding.' Her parents can look after him, the plan being that we stay with them on Saturday night. 'They really want to meet you both.'

'You've told them about Doggo?'

'Of course,' she replies. 'You're not the only one I share an office with.'

I lie, tell her I'm free at the weekend.

J will be furious with me, but I'm not going to pass up the chance of a weekend in the country with Edie. Besides, J is already furious with me. He blames me for Lily leaving him. It happened a few nights ago – a blazing row about nothing in particular, as is their way, but this time there was no tearful reconciliation. Lily threw her wine glass at the flat-screen TV, packed a bag and took a cab to her sister's place. She says it's over – which of course it isn't – and J is convinced that Clara and I are responsible, that our split was the catalyst. It's possible. I've seen it before, the domino effect: one relationship falls, then others start to tumble, as if some sacred taboo has been broken and all bets are suddenly off. I don't hold myself to blame, and I don't suppose J really expects me to. What he wants from me is company on Saturday night.

In its own slightly sick way, it's an inspired idea. I mean, who in their right mind would pick Heathrow Airport for a wild night out? Answer: a man who travels extensively for work and knows that the hotels serving major airports are jammed with long-haul stewardesses on stopover. 'Never call them steward-esses, they don't like that. They're flight attendants.' They may be too tired to schlep into central London, but that doesn't mean they're not looking to have a good time. 'Think about it – the parking's free and the room's already paid for.'

I laughed, found myself saying yes, and ever since have been searching for an excuse to duck out. I now have it.

Fat Trev, or what remains of him, opens the door of his flat in a tight black T-shirt and with a Maximuscle protein shake in his hand. He's almost unrecognisable. Making a positive ID isn't helped by the fact that he has also shaved off his bushy beard (possibly because he now has a jawline to show to the world).

'Jesus Christ, Trev, what happened to the other half of you?'

I'm expecting a laugh, or at least a smile. I get a ridiculously firm handshake and 'It's my new HIIT routine.'

'HIIT?'

'High Intensity Interval Training.'

'Oh, right.'

'Come in.'

As I step past him, I mentally cross ballet-dancing hippos off the list of amusing topics for discussion.

His flat has been stripped back to basics, and there's a rowing machine in the middle of the living room. He's friendly enough at first, sympathetic about Clara, and grateful that I've made the effort to tell him in person about my new job at Indology, although it turns out he'd already got wind of it from someone.

'I'm cool with it,' he says, handing me a mug of green tea. 'Completely cool.'

It's not a great restaurant, but it's the only place near Trev's flat that accepts dogs, and at least it spares us a meal at the vegan café he initially had in mind for us. He may have given up wheat and dairy, but alcohol is still on the menu. Not at first, not until I make the mistake of ordering a second gin and tonic and he decides to abandon the San Pellegrino and keep me company.

We chat a lot about him, about how much he has changed, how much he has learned about himself, how he has grown as a person even as his body has been shrinking. This is the sort of talk that sets alarm bells ringing with me – maybe now more than ever, now that Clara is gone and I don't have to listen to tales of personal improvement all the time

– but I manage to make the right noises, or at least I think I do: 'That's very interesting, Trev . . . I'd never thought of it like that . . . You're right, how can you possibly love someone else if you don't love yourself?'

The truth is, though, I've never really got the whole self-love thing. The people I most respect tend to have a remarkably low opinion of themselves, a keen sense of their own foolishness and fallibility. I don't say this to Trev, but he obviously picks up on something in my tone or my expression.

'You're such a bloody cynic, Dan.'

'No I'm not.'

'You always were.'

'You didn't do too badly on that front yourself.'

'Yeah, and look where it got me. Watch your step.'

'Thanks for your concern, Trev. I'll be fine.'

'Maybe. I just hope you find the balls to ring some changes.'

'Like you, you mean?'

Trev tops up his wine glass and leans closer, a demented gleam in his eye. 'It's mouthwash, Dan – fucking mouthwash.'

'You're wrong. It's also hair colourant, and there's talk of a TV ad for an ugly French hatchback.'

'Go ahead, laugh it off if you want, but it's peddling crap to the masses. You really want to spend the rest of your life doing that?'

That's when he kicks off in earnest, tearing into the industry, and into me for being a spineless lackey who anaesthetises himself with dreams of a novel he's never going to write.

I'm looking at him and I'm thinking that I don't much like the new moob-free, quinoa-munching, gym-addicted Trev, and I know that any second now I'm going to start returning fire. I don't, though, because as I'm about to, Doggo shifts at my feet and I feel the warm pressure of his body against my leg. It's not like him – he's not big on physical overtures – and as I'm pondering this, the moment passes, my rising anger mysteriously fading away.

So I sit there and take it – no easy thing when someone's talking utter crap, but a whole lot harder when they're piling on some painful home truths.

Chapter Fifteen

'I'LL BE RIGHT down,' comes Edie's voice over the intercom, disappointingly. I would have liked to see her flat, glimpse how she and Douglas live. If her desk is anything to go by, it'll be tidy, ordered. I see white walls, wooden floorboards and magazines piled on a retro glass coffee table. Douglas is a banker, and in my experience bankers like their homes to have a whiff of scrubbed sterility. They don't want brown furniture and threadbare Turkish rugs and wallpaper and arcane objects gathering dust on marble mantelpieces; they want clean, hard lines and big TVs and big fridges with not much in them.

I've offered to drive, which has meant giving the car its first good clean in more than a year, inside and out. I've even spread a blanket on the back seat for Doggo to lie on. He only knows Edie in a work context and I can see the confusion in his eyes as we load her bag into the boot. He senses something special is afoot.

Everyone thinks they're a great driver, or so it's said. I don't. I know I'm too slow for most people's tastes, and I don't take any pride in fighting my way through city traffic. Skipping between lanes in order to buy a place or two in the tailback from the next red light has always struck me as a pointless exercise. I'm happy to pootle along, making way for those who are clearly in more of a hurry than I am.

'Don't mention it!' snaps Edie when I let a BMW out of a side street and the man at the wheel doesn't acknowledge my kindness. 'He could have thanked you.'

'Edie, it's the weekend, the sun is shining, Adele is singing to us.'

'It's the principle. Common courtesy.'

'We have it, he doesn't. Who cares? Relax.'

'You're right,' she says. 'Here! Turn left, I know a short cut through Barons Court.'

We spend the next twenty minutes mired in roadworks in Barons Court with a bunch of other people who know Edie's short cut.

I've been to Henley once before, to watch a girl I fancied at university row in a regatta. I remember it as an attractive town set on a bend in the Thames, with a slightly smug air of prosperity about it. It hasn't changed much in the past decade. We're worming our way round the one-way system when Edie drops the bombshell.

'There's something you should know. Douglas doesn't exist.'

It takes me a moment to find the words. 'That's not creepy.'

'I mean, he exists, it's just we haven't been together for a bit.'

'How long's a bit?'

'Eight months.'

She says she kept the news from people at work because it's easier to be thought of as in a relationship when you're not looking for another one. Meanwhile, I'm thinking, *I bet Tristan knows. In fact, I wouldn't be surprised if he insisted she end it with Douglas.* I'm also thinking about the many lies she has spun me over the past weeks: the talk of pool practice with Douglas at her local pub, and the touching little details of their relationship, the way he sweetly consoled her when she cried at the cinema last week, the surprise dinner at the Michelin-starred restaurant after we won SWOSH!. Bullshit, all of it. I'm obviously wearing these thoughts on my face.

'Don't be angry with me. You should try being a single girl. It can be oppressive.'

'I'm not angry with you.'

'Dan, look at me.'

'I can't, I might crash into the back of that Range Rover. Jesus, doesn't anyone here drive a normal car?'

'My parents do, and theirs is even crappier than yours.' We trade a conciliatory look. 'I didn't need to tell you,' she says.

'Yes you did. You're briefing me for later.'

'True, but I didn't have to invite you in the first place.'

'Why did you?'

'Because I'm sick of lying to you.'

For a moment I think she's about to unburden herself further, possibly bring up Tristan, but she steers the conversation back to her parents, warning me that they're a little odd. 'And the house is a tip. Don't bank on fresh linen and flowers in your room. It's not how they do things. In fact, they've probably forgotten we're coming.'

They live beyond Henley, high in the Chiltern hills, which I don't know, and which seem improbably wild and under-populated for somewhere so close to London. This is where

Edie grew up, in an old stone house on the fringes of a hamlet that sits at the head of a broad valley studded with tall trees and grazing cattle. It's like something out of a Thomas Hardy novel – the bucolic idyll, the rustic utopia (before Mr Hardy takes his scalpel to it).

They haven't forgotten we're coming. Her father, Elliot, greets us in the gravel driveway. He's a tall man with a shock of thick hair that shoots off in all directions, as befits a composer. He's wearing a pair of ancient draw-string rugby shorts and, bizarrely, a faded Blue Oyster Cult T-shirt.

'Papa, you're bleeding.'

It's true; he is. There are scratches all over his arms, some of them quite deep.

'Your mother's had me clearing brambles all morning.'

'Where is she?'

'God knows. Throwing a pot, probably.' He grips my hand. 'Excuse my ill-mannered daughter. You must be David.'

'Daniel.'

'Forgive me. No head for names. Or faces, if the truth be told.' When he makes to hug Edie, she fends him off, worried about her white shirt.

'Papa, the blood . . .'

They make do with extended necks and a kiss on both cheeks. 'Looking more beautiful than ever, my darling.' He drops to his long haunches to greet Doggo. 'And you, my little friend, are considerably more ugly than I was led to believe.'

Her mother is indeed throwing a pot. We find her in a converted pigsty that now serves as her studio. Her name is Sibella, and I can see immediately where Edie gets her large and slightly feline eyes from. Sibella's raven-coloured hair is threaded with silver and heaped on top of her head, held in place by what look like a couple of chopsticks.

'Darling,' she says with a swift glance, her foot pumping the pedal, spinning the wheel. 'Daniel, Doggo, welcome. Now bugger off, all of you. I'm at a critical point.'

The house isn't exactly a tip, but the downstairs rooms do have a junk shop quality to them. There are books everywhere, bowing the built-in shelves, which fight for wall space with glazed cabinets stuffed with curios of all kinds, most of it of an archaeological nature: fragments of earthenware pots, bronze figurines, fossils and the like. The flagged kitchen is cathedral cold, even on a day like this. The run of quality pans dangling from hooks declares it to be the HQ of a foodie household, as does the armoury of knives stuck to the long magnetic strip on the wall beside the Aga. The music room overlooking the back garden contains the largest collection of vinyl I've seen outside of a second-hand record shop. A grand piano, lid down and loaded with sheet music, holds centre stage, but there are other instruments scattered about the place, as if the musicians had downed tools suddenly and shot off as one for a loo break.

'Do you play the piano?' I ask.

'Yes.'

'The cello?' It's propped against a faded peach-velvet divan.

'Uh-huh.'

I point. 'The harp?'

'A little.'

'No way.'

'It's true.'

'Prove it.'

Edie takes a seat and tilts the enormous instrument back against her shoulder. I watch, mesmerised, as her long fingers flutter around the strings, not appearing to touch them. A little for her is evidently a lot by anyone else's standards; that's clear even to me, with my tin ear and my zero talent for music. I've heard the piece before but can't place it.

'Debussy's first Arabesque,' says Edie when she's done. 'It's easier to play than it sounds, but don't tell anyone.'

My low, beamed bedroom is just down the corridor from hers. We meet briefly in the bathroom, she in her navy blue linen dress, me in my suit, she to fiddle with her hair and apply some make-up, me to adjust the knot of my tie and dab at an old stain on my lapel with a wet flannel.

We just have time for a quick chat and a glass of Prosecco with Elliot and Sibella on the back terrace, where a toast is raised to our recent success. 'Does she really have what it takes?' asks Sibella, in that way that only mothers can.

'In spades,' I reply.

'You *will* look after her, won't you?'

'If she needs me to, but I'm not sure she does.'

'It's a big bad world out there.'

'Mum . . .' groans Edie.

'It's true,' insists Sibella. 'And success always come at a price.'

'Yes, take it from us,' chips in Elliot with a wry chuckle. I opt for a plastered smile, thrown by the self-deprecation (could my own father ever have uttered such a line?) but also uneasy with the idea of laughing along at the failed aspirations of my hosts.

Elliot runs us to the pub in their ancient Golf, which is indeed even more decrepit than my Peugeot, with some impressive dents and a stereo system that harks back to a time when cassettes were the very height of in-car entertainment. The village where the wedding is taking place lies ten minutes away down sun-dappled country lanes bursting with new growth. It's hard to imagine a more perfect day on which to get married – not quite hot enough to raise a sweat, and with big cotton-wool clouds passing by high overhead like galleons in full sail.

The groom, Jeremy/Jez/Jezza (buzz cut and diamond stud earring), has shoved a bundle of cash behind the bar at the Royal Oak. He's the oldest brother of Edie's best friend when she was growing up, a loud girl with a platinum-blond bob called Trisha/Trish, whose boyfriend Richard/Rick/Dickster is a cousin of Edie's first ever boyfriend, Alex/Al, a short, handsome, nervy fellow who offers me a limp hand and a hostile glare when I'm introduced to him in the beer garden out back. He only begins to relax once he's figured that Edie and I aren't an item, just work colleagues.

It's a short stroll up the high street from the pub to the church. We find a space in the sea of hats and hushed conversations. The bride shows up suitably late in a bustled and beaded triumph of excess which no self-respecting fairy would be seen dead in. Tears well in Edie's eyes during the opening hymn. 'She had such a tough time when we were younger,' she whispers to me.

A huge cheer goes up when Jez finally gets to kiss the meringue he has just married, and five minutes later we're pelting them with rice in the churchyard. It's only my third wedding, but I already know this isn't how I'll end up tying the knot. Inevitably, my thoughts turn to Clara. We sometimes discussed how we'd do it. Clara imagined some exotic location, a humanistic ceremony on a beach or clifftop with a handful of close friends as witnesses, which was fine by me, although a larger gathering at Chelsea Registry Office followed by a blow-out feast in a nearby restaurant would have got my vote too. Not that it matters any more.

That's the thing about weddings: they stir up memories, not all of them good. They also stir up trouble. Looking around, I see a number of young men in their twenties standing awkwardly beside their girlfriends, avoiding the looks that say, 'And what about us?' I also spot Alex sneaking a cigarette by the lychgate. He's staring intently at Edie, who's deep in conversation with a wizened old bird teetering on two walking sticks, and I have the uneasy feeling that I'm going to have to keep an eye on him later.

Edie cadges us a lift to the stately home turned country hotel where the party is taking place. It's a sprawling Georgian pile set in glorious grounds. I don't expect her to nanny me, and she clearly has no plans to, losing herself in the throng on the back terrace, searching out old faces. There's a lot to be said for a social gathering where you don't know a soul: there's no one you need to avoid, and it's possible to walk away from a dull conversation without causing too much offence. I drift around, following my nose, which leads me to the far end of the lawn and a tall girl in a floppy straw hat who's smoking a spliff behind a sculpture of a lion attacking a horse.

'Police,' I say.

'Let's see your badge.'

'I'm undercover. And I'm going to need that as evidence.'

She hands me the spliff. I take a drag. 'Yep, it's the real deal. You're busted.'

'So will you be after two more tokes.' She's not joking; it's elephant strength. Twenty minutes later, when a preposterous little man dressed like a town crier summons everyone inside the marquee for dinner, I still don't know her name, and I don't ask. It would spoil the moment.

I've had my phone off since entering the church; I now fire it up as I'm checking the seating plan. There's a voicemail from my mother. I can tell immediately that she's been crying. Alcohol probably accounts for the slight slurring.

'Danny, sweetpea, it's me. Call me when you can. It's important.'

I try to remember the last time she called me 'sweetpea', and I see a boy with a side parting in grey corduroy shorts. A cold hand clutches at my heart. I have a pretty good idea what the message means. If something had happened to Nigel – and let's face it, a heart attack or stroke isn't out of the question, given how he carries on – she would have said so. No, this is something between us, something she wants to share in real time.

'Shit,' I mumble.

'You should see who *I'm* sitting next to,' jokes the old boy at my shoulder.

The food and wine are excellent, unlike the speeches. The bride's stepfather keeps mentioning how much the bash is costing him, Jez abandons his notes and gets way too graphic about his new wife's gifts between the sheets, then the best man and the best woman go for a scripted double act with a load of ba-dum-tsshh gags, most of which fall flat.

Edie fires me a look full of apology, and I wonder why she really invited me. She must have known I wouldn't go down a storm with the likes of her great pal Trisha, who took one look at me and said to herself the same thing I said to myself: not my type at all.

Clara used to dance as if in a trance, as though all the forces of Mother Nature were rising up through the soles of her feet, animating her limbs. Unfortunately, I've picked up something of this look: head back, eyes closed, arms raised, swaying like seaweed caught in a cross-current. I know it's not a good look, but lost in the throes of a club remix of David Bowie's 'Heroes', it makes perfect sense to me. I'm there. Everyone else is only close. Keep up if you can.

'Are you all right?' Edie shouts in my ear.

I open my eyes to see her looking mildly concerned. 'I've got some other moves but I'm holding them back.'

'That sounds wise,' she quips.

'Someone once said, "dance like nobody's watching".'

'But they are.'

It's true, they are. There are even a couple of kids mimicking me.

'Emulation is the highest form of flattery,' I shout back above the music.

'Who said that?'

'Fuck knows. Who cares?'

That's when I realise I'm drunk, and that I need another drink. I head outside with a vodka and tonic from the bar. It's almost midnight in Spain, but that's okay. Mum's a night owl; she'll still be up, waiting for me to phone her back. I dial, then immediately kill the call. I'm sober enough (just) to have the conversation, but I don't want to, not right now. No, what I want is to spend one more night as me, as Daniel

Wynne, son of Michael Wynne and Ann Wynne (née Larssen), brother to Emma, not half-brother. The sky is bright with stars, but I can sense my mood beginning to darken so I head back into the marquee in search of distraction. It comes in the form of a large and well-spoken woman in a taffeta dress who flops down beside me at the empty table I've installed myself at. She's sweating from her recent exertions on the dance floor.

'You should be out there,' she announces, pouring herself a glass of white wine.

'Excuse me?'

'Defending your claim.' She nods towards the dance floor, where Edie is gyrating with three blokes, one of whom is Alex.

'We're not together. We just work together.'

'How boring.'

I can't claim to know the countryside well, but I did grow up in Norwich, a city surrounded by wild swathes of the stuff, so I feel safe in saying that country people are utterly unlike city people. It's nothing as obvious as having a shotgun or two tucked under your bed; it's what they do with their time, how they go about putting bread on the table. You meet people who make a living from dredging ditches or thatching roofs or fixing dry-stone walls or neutering cattle or servicing farm machinery or selling fertiliser. Barbara in the taffeta dress stables other people's horses for a living, although she also breeds ponies on the side. That's how she fills her waking hours, that's how she fills the tank of her 'shit-covered Land Rover'. She's a close friend of the bride's mother. She also taught Edie to ride, 'many moons ago now'.

'Don't tell me, she was a natural.'

'Of course. Things have always come easily to Edie. Except . . .' She trails off.

'What?'

'It's not my place to say.'

I slide my hand inside my jacket. 'I'll pay you.'

Barbara smiles. 'Keep your money, it's on me.' Then, after a slug of wine: 'One word. Love.'

'Love?'

'She's always looked for it in the wrong place.'

'And where's the right place?'

'Anywhere you're not searching for it.' I weigh these words of wisdom. 'Don't look so impressed,' she says. 'I got it from *Cosmopolitan*. Full of nonsense, that magazine. You know the sort of thing – "Are you a red, green or blue woman?"'

'Which one are you?'

'Me? I'm a happily married woman who's also been happily divorced twice, so what do I know about anything?'

'Much more than you're letting on, I suspect.'

She shrugs the flattery aside. 'Are you a homosexual?'

'Promise not to lynch me if I say yes?'

She gives an affronted gasp. 'Excuse me! We're not as backward as you city types like to think. In fact, we're really quite liberal. We have to be. There's no keeping secrets in a place like this.'

'No, I'm not a homosexual.'

'So why aren't you out there fighting for her?' Another nod towards the dance floor. 'I mean, look at her. Don't tell me you can't see it. She's ravishing, and that's not a word I'd use of many people.'

'I spend all day in an office with her. Could you live and work with the same person?'

'Oh, you old romantic.'

'Could you?'

'You don't deserve her if that's your attitude.'

'Well, could you?'

She ignores the question again. 'Just find a way to make it work, or learn to live with the regret.' She lays a hand on my forearm. 'No job is for life; love can be.'

'*Cosmopolitan* again?'

'No, I think that one might have been *Grazia*.'

Things start to go wrong the moment Barbara's husband whisks her away to meet someone. Desperate for a piss, I'm heading for the exit when I see Edie gesturing for me to come and dance, an invitation that doesn't go down too well with Alex, judging from his scowl. I signal that I'll be right back, but I haven't banked on the queue for the gents, and it's at least ten minutes before I return. The first thing I see on entering the marquee is Edie turning away from Alex and him seizing her by the arm and yanking her back. Before I know it, I'm right beside them on the dance floor.

'Everything okay?'

Edie is looking shaken, upset. 'Yeah.'

Alex is looking drunk and defiant. 'All good.'

'No, not good,' I say. 'Putting your hands on a woman.'

'She never had a problem with my hands on her before.'

It's a horrible line, smug, suggestive, possessive, and I can feel myself squaring up to him.

'Dan, let it go,' says Edie.

'Yeah, Dan, let it go,' sneers Alex. 'In fact, why don't you just fuck off?'

'Don't push your luck, you little prick.'

He takes a step back. 'I'm a black belt in karate.'

'Hold the front page: small man into martial arts discovered.'

For a worrying moment I think I might have misjudged him, but he knows better than to ruin Jez and Amy's special day with a dance floor brawl. He spins on his heel and stomps off.

Edie looks aghast. 'I can't believe you did that.'

'What, I should have waited till he slapped you around a bit?'

She hurries off after Alex. As I make for the bar, I find myself squeezing past Barbara. She has obviously witnessed what happened, because she winks at me and says, 'Now that's more like it.'

The taxi ride back to her parents' place is fifteen minutes of frosty silence. Edie only speaks once I've paid off the driver and we've let ourselves into the kitchen through the back door.

'Nightcap?' she asks.

'Why not?'

I'm in the doghouse, we might as well get it over with, clear the air to spare her parents any tensions tomorrow. She produces a bottle of Armagnac from somewhere and we dump ourselves at the kitchen table.

'Edie, I'm sorry.'

'It's a bit late for sorrys.'

'They do tend to come after the event,' I point out.

'It was nothing I couldn't deal with. I certainly didn't need you turning into Rambo.'

'I didn't like him manhandling you. I couldn't help myself.'

She shakes her head. 'I should never have invited you.'

That hurts. I can feel my hackles rising. 'Yeah, well we both know why you did.'

'Do we?'

It came to me suddenly in the taxi just now: I'm the decoy to draw attention away from her and Tristan. There was gossip in the office yesterday about the two of us spending the weekend together.

'Was it your idea or Tristan's?' I ask.

'Tristan? What's Tristan got to do with anything?'

It's a pretty convincing performance, and I take a slow sip of Armagnac, stretching out the silence. 'Forget it.'

'No, I want to know what you mean. Tell me what you mean.'

'I mean, I wasn't sure about you and him before, but now I am.'

I'm expecting a fight to the death, but she throws in the towel almost immediately, not with words but with a low sigh and eyes that can't hold mine.

'I'm not judging you, Edie.'

'Yeah, that would be a bit rich coming from the bloke who screwed his girlfriend's sister.'

I'm liable to say something she'll never forget or forgive me for, so I wait a moment before replying. 'You can have that one on me if it makes you feel better.'

She hangs her head. 'No. Christ, what a cow.'

I reach over and squeeze her hand. 'We don't have to talk about it now. In fact, I don't think we should.'

'What if I want to?'

'Sleep on it. My head's all over the shop – family stuff, not this.'

'Nothing serious, I hope.'

'No,' I lie.

We part company in the gloom at the foot of the staircase because I want to check on Doggo in the drawing room.

'Small man into martial arts discovered,' she says. I can just make out her smile.

'Like that, did you?'

'Not at the time.' She plants an unexpected kiss on my cheek. 'Thanks for coming to my defence.'

'One day I'll figure you out,' I say to her back as she heads upstairs.

'Don't be so sure,' she replies from the darkness.

Doggo is slumbering on the sofa in the drawing room. He stirs as I approach.

'Hey, Doggo, how's tricks?' I drop down beside him. I can feel a couple of burrs in the long hair of his ears. They suggest that Elliot and Sibella were true to their word and took him for a long yomp through the countryside. 'Run you ragged, did they?'

Doggo shadows me as I leave the room, and when I close the door on him he barks, then again, and again. 'Shhhh,' I hiss, easing open the door. He barges through the crack into the corridor, wagging his bog brush tail and looking up at me with doleful eyes.

'You want company? Okay, but just this once.'

Doggo sleeps. I don't. I lie there on my back, feeling the weight of him through the duvet, pressing against my thigh.

He must find it as reassuring as I do, because when I move my leg, he shifts to maintain contact. It occurs to me that maybe he was used to this – sleeping on the bed of his last owner – and it's taken him until now to feel comfortable enough with me to demand the same. He twitches, gives a little whinny, dreaming. Of what? His former life?

It's odd that I haven't stopped to think about it before. What do I really know about his past? Only what Clara told me, that he wasn't a stray, that he came from a good home, a happy home. This makes sense. There's nothing cringing, fearful or damaged about him. He's not a needy dog, one of those irritating creatures that shiver with the anticipation of receiving even the slightest attention. Yes, he's happy to be petted but just as happy to fire you a sharp look when he's had enough. I respect him for that. He's his own man, self-possessed but never to the point of arrogance, aware of his intelligence but not quick to flaunt it, and he's sweetly deluded about the figure he cuts in the world. If I had to pick a character from literature to compare him to, it would be Hercule Poirot.

Hercule. Finally! A fitting name for the little fellow. The French form, mind, not the English one. Hercules summons up images of the Greek hero and his twelve labours, with their feats of courage and strength – two characteristics I don't immediately associate with Doggo. *Hercule*. Yes. But still not quite as good as Doggo.

I lay my hand on him as softly as I can so as not to wake him. The heat and the slow, hypnotic rise and fall of his ribcage carry me quickly off to the same place he has gone.

Chapter Sixteen

WE EAT BREAKFAST in blinding sunshine on the back terrace. It's exhausting, not just the spread, but the conversation, which is diverse, lively, even argumentative. Elliot tosses out stories from the Sunday papers and everyone is expected to react to them. Another drone strike in northern Pakistan has obliterated a bunch of innocents. What do we think about drones? Is the war against the Taliban really a war? What defines a just war? Is there even such a thing? What are we to make of man's inhumanity to man?

'And beast,' says Sibella, a vegetarian, although she doesn't seem to have a problem with the rest of us piling into the platter of bacon, sausages and black pudding.

More coffee is made. The conversation turns to me. Not quite an interrogation, but close. I don't know why I do it – I mean, I hardly know these people – yet out it pops: Grandpa's line to me in the nursing home, my mother's stiff rebuttal, then the cryptic voicemail from her on my phone last night.

'It's probably nothing,' is Edie's verdict.

Sibella frowns. 'Poor you.'

I shrug, trying to make light of it. 'It's not so bad. You don't know my father.'

'Neither do you, it seems,' says Elliot.

'Papa!'

'I'm just trying to inject a bit of levity.'

At the bottom of the garden is a rickety bench with its back to a brick wall trained with an ancient rose on the point of flowering, loaded with fat buds. My eye takes in all the details, forensically, like a detective visiting a crime scene for the first time. This is the spot where the world as I know it is about to change for ever, and it's good to have Doggo sitting beside me on the bench.

Nigel answers after several rings. 'Hold on a tick, old boy, she's right here,' he says in his faux-patrician drawl. I can tell they're outside, probably by the pool, cooking themselves to a crisp under a Spanish sun.

'Danny. Finally. You got my message?'

'Sorry, my phone was off, I was at a wedding.'

She wants to know whose wedding, and where exactly in the Chilterns I am, and whether this means there's something brewing between Edie and me. Her questions don't have the ring of an awkward preamble, of someone steeling herself to raise the real and rather sticky item on the agenda. She sounds genuinely curious, chatty, and in the end I'm the one to remind her: 'Mum, you said it was important.'

'Oh. Yes. It is. I can't find my birthday diary and I know Alice's is coming up soon. Emma will kill me if I forget it again.'

I don't reply.

'Danny, are you there?'

'You sounded upset.'

'Upset?'

'In your message. Like you'd been crying.'

It turns out she had been, having just received news that an old friend of hers had lost her battle with breast cancer. 'You remember Pat Connelly.' Vaguely. I see a wide face and a cascade of dark curls from my childhood. 'I'm waiting to hear when the funeral is. Maybe we can have lunch when I'm over for it.'

'Sure. Sure.'

'I'm touched by your enthusiasm,' she jokes.

I can't bring myself to tell the others the truth. They'll think I'm a paranoiac (am I?), or worse – a fantasist. I go for the big fudge, not quite a lie. 'She's flying over soon. She wants to have lunch with me.'

'That's all she said?' asks Sibella, her eyes boring into me.

'Yes.'

'No sense of whether you're right or not?'

'Sib, leave the poor boy alone,' says Elliot. 'Can't you see he doesn't want to talk about it.'

'He was happy enough to talk about it before.'

Edie skewers her mother with a look. Sibella lets it go, but I can tell she smells a rat.

I told Edie to sleep on it, and she has. The subject of Tristan is now off limits. We're well on our way back to London when I finally broach it.

'What's to say? It is what it is.'

'Edie, he's married.'

'Unhappily married. And you said you wouldn't judge me.'

'I'm not judging you, I'm just . . .' I can't find the word.
'What?'
'I don't know. Worried, I suppose.'
'You don't have to be.'
And that's that – end of conversation.

Chapter Seventeen

I't's good to have Ralph back at the helm. Yes, there's something vaguely ridiculous about him, a whiff of Captain Jack Sparrow, but at least he commands respect, unlike Tristan, who demands it. Tristan is right in my sights now. It was never exactly possible to ignore him before, but I was able to push him to the periphery. No longer, not since I got the confirmation about him and Edie. I can tell he's not happy about having to play second fiddle once more; it's written in his eyes when Ralph is briefing us all on the Vargo account.

The Vargo is the new hatchback from . . . well, it's anybody's guess; we're not allowed to know just which of the Big Three French carmakers is responsible for it. The invitation to pitch for the TV ad has come via a brand and marketing consultancy whose client wishes the competing agencies to approach the matter without any preconceptions, with nothing but the merits of the vehicle itself to work with. There is only one problem: said merits are encased within the Vargo, a vehicle that's best described as wilfully ugly – a snub-nosed, boxy affair that flies in the face of current trends in automotive design. Yes, it's got great fuel economy and a whole bunch of gadgets as standard, but it's an aberration, an ungainly lump of metal for the conveyance of passengers from A to B.

'Who would want to buy it?' asks Ralph.

'Who indeed?' says Tristan.

'Some dipstick with more money than sense,' suggests Megan.

There are eleven of us around the conference table: the three creative teams, Patrick, a couple of other account executives (Damien and Lotty), plus Ralph and Tristan. A TV commercial for a new vehicle launch would be a big feather in the cap of a small agency like ours, but Tristan thinks we should leave it well alone. He's convinced the Vargo is doomed, not just to failure but ridicule. Do we really want to be associated with it?

'Defeatist crap!' scoffs Ralph. 'Anyone can sell the new BMW 5 Series – that's just following tracks in the snow. But the person who finds a market for this piece of shit, well, that's how lasting reputations are built. Damn it, we'll still be dining out on it in our nursing homes if we pull it off.'

There's a nervous edge to the chuckle that ripples round the table, because Tristan has a face like thunder. '"If" being the operative word. I still think it's a poisoned chalice.'

'Objection duly noted,' says Ralph. 'I want you all on it. Answers on a postcard by Wednesday week, please.'

Tristan's public dressing-down is a source of amused discussion once we're all gathered round the pool table back in the creative department. I find myself sympathising with him, chiefly for Edie's sake, because it can't be easy to hear the man you're sleeping with being vilified with such casual relish by your colleagues. Later, when we're alone in our office, Edie tells me she doesn't need me fighting Tristan's corner, even if she can't.

I don't appreciate my good intentions being trashed. 'How about you tell me what to say and I'll say it?'

'Or you could just say what you really think.'

'You don't want to hear what I really think.'

The truth is, and despite what I told her before, I *do* judge her. Not morally, more on grounds of taste.

'You only see one face,' says Edie.

'How many does he have?'

'Screw you, Dan.'

Doggo barks suddenly from the sofa, as if sensing the tension and calling us both to order. We glance at him, look at each other and smile. It's good to have an excuse to put the sour exchange behind us.

'Maybe you'll change your mind about him after your lunch tomorrow.'

I'd completely forgotten until Tristan mentioned it earlier. He has booked us a table at a swanky new brasserie in Covent Garden, which is a bummer, because I haven't forgotten that I promised to pay, and I don't suppose he has either.

It's a prime table right in the heart of the restaurant, a padded booth for two. I've made a point of rereading the chapter Tristan gave me, and there's no denying it: the guy can write. The tone is perfectly pitched. There's a lightness of touch, but nothing so frothy that it undermines the authority of his message.

Tristan seems genuinely grateful for the praise, and he's

thrilled with the tag-line I've come up with for the title: *De-Management: A Science of Less Is More for Big Business*.

'I've been set on the word "theory",' he tells me. 'But "science" packs more of a punch.' He also likes the phrase 'big business', because that's the crowd he feels he's speaking to.

Our food arrives ridiculously late, but he's very sweet with our browbeaten waitress. He knows she's not to blame; the fault lies with the kitchen. It turns out he put himself through university waiting tables, and I'm beginning to warm to him, beginning to understand what Edie sees in him, when he comes out with it. He's nothing if not direct, but even by his standards it's one hell of a line.

'If you fuck her, I'll fire you.'

'Sorry?'

'You heard me. Edie.'

'I've got to admit, I never read the small print. Is that in my contract?'

'Don't bother,' he says with a tight smile. 'I know you know about us.'

And I know he's bluffing, because Edie assured me earlier she hasn't said anything to him.

'Well I do now.'

'You did before. She let it slip over the weekend, or you got it out of her. It doesn't matter how it happened. What matters is I mean it.'

'Tristan, I don't want to sleep with her.'

'Of course you do. Everyone does.'

'I doubt Patrick does.'

He doesn't appreciate my feeble stab at humour. 'I mean it. What the right hand giveth, the left hand can take away.'

'Not without Ralph's consent,' I reply feebly.

'Ralph's not in a position to disagree.'

'Oh?'

Tristan savours a sip of his coffee. 'Put it this way, Indology is going places, but not necessarily with Ralph.'

'Meaning?'

'Meaning that's off the record, for your ears only.'

I've underestimated him, his hubris, his hunger for power. He doesn't just want a seat at the table, he wants the one at the head of it. If there was any doubt, he now starts talking about the outmoded structure of the company and about his vision of a leaner, looser outfit, more like a cooperative, with the key players holding shares. And as he rattles on, I wonder if this was the same offer he made to Edie: come fly with me to the stars, oh, and get rich in the process.

He hasn't forgotten I'm paying for lunch, and as soon as I've called for the tab, I head for the toilets. I don't really need to go; I just want some privacy to fire off a text to Edie: *Beware! He knows I know*

Tristan is downstairs, waiting for my answer. He hasn't actually spelled out a deal, but it's pretty clear he's sweetening the threats with promises, buying my silence about Edie and my support against Ralph. I'm staggered by his behaviour. Doesn't it matter to him that I know he's an unfaithful husband? Not if it helps bind me to his cause. Doesn't he care what people in the industry will say about him muscling Ralph out? Not if he manages to pull off his palace coup. It's impressive to witness such blind ambition in action, but it *is* blind.

I'm almost insulted that he has misjudged me so badly. He isn't to know I'm disenchanted with the industry, looking for a way out, but didn't he stop, even for a moment, to think that I might fight him on principle? What really gets my goat, though, is that if he's ready to destroy me, then he's ready to destroy Edie too. And I'm never going to let him do that.

Returning to the table, I glance at the bill now waiting for me. 'Count me in,' I say.

'Good boy.'

He grins, and I want to punch him in his perfect teeth.

Edie's not around when Tristan and I get back from lunch. She and Anna have taken Doggo off for a treat. Apparently the office postman has learned a couple of new names and earned himself a reward as a result. I hear this from Josh, who collars me as I'm passing through the design department.

'The weird thing is, he knows Megan's name but he still won't deliver to her.'

'Go figure,' chortles Eric from his desk.

Josh has had a shot at drawing up the comic strip I mentioned to him last week. This has nothing to do with work; it's just an old idea of mine that's been knocking around for a bit.

'Josh, this is genius.'

'Nah, something's missing.'

Josh isn't exactly a frustrated artist; he's a very good one who has figured (rightly) that the only way to get a mortgage is to have a salaried job. Abstract oil painting is his thing, but he's also a gifted caricaturist, something I only realised when I spotted him doodling on a pad in a meeting.

He has nailed the idea in three deftly drawn frames. The first shows a baby in a high chair flanked by his parents, who are feeding him. The baby is trying to speak: 'M-m-m-m . . .'

'His first word's going to be Mummy!' declares the delighted mother. In frame two, the baby is stammering 'D-d-d-d . . .' and the father is now looking thrilled: 'No, it's going to be Daddy!' In the third and final frame, baby blurts out: 'McDonald's!'

'Nothing's missing,' I tell Josh. 'It's spot on.'

Everything's perfect: the food spraying from baby's mouth in the last frame, the look of wild delight on his face, the look of utter dejection on his parents', all conveyed with the barest strokes of a pen. Eric thinks we should send it off to a newspaper or magazine, possibly *Private Eye*. Josh vetoes the idea, though not on principle. It can go out when he's happy with it.

Doggo's treat from the girls turns out to be a wash, cut and blow dry at a pet grooming place near Charlotte Street. He has never looked so good and he knows it, parading around the offices on his return, head held high, fielding the compliments. I experience a twinge of possessiveness. I'm happy that he has wormed his way into other people's affections over the past weeks, but I can't help thinking that my own relationship with him is beginning to suffer as a result. He's even loath to have one of our romps on the sofa, possibly because he doesn't want me mussing up his new coiffure. However, his irritation with me isn't a patch on Edie's, as becomes clear the moment we find ourselves alone.

'I can't believe you told him you knew about us!' She means Tristan and the text I sent her from the restaurant.

'I didn't tell him.'

'Well I sure as hell didn't.'

'Edie, calm down. He guessed. I don't know how. And anyway, he didn't seem to mind too much.'

'That's rubbish. He's paranoid about people finding out.'

'Well he doesn't have to worry. Nor do you. I won't tell a soul.'

She dumps herself at her desk with a sigh. 'I hate you knowing. You'll be watching me like a hawk now.'

'Then you shouldn't have told me.'

'I didn't! You forced it out of me.'

'Hardly. You folded without a fight.'

'True,' she says. 'I must be losing my touch.'

Chapter Eighteen

THE FIRST I know of it is when Ralph appears at my shoulder and asks me to follow him. It's a short stroll from our office to Megan and Seth's, where the reason for Ralph's scowling silence soon becomes clear.

It's sitting on the carpet, right by Megan's desk.

'Ah,' I say, stooping to examine it.

'It's dog shit,' says Megan, glowering at me from the safety of an armchair.

'Are you sure?'

'What, you think Seth did it?'

I glance enquiringly at Seth, who holds up his hands in a gesture of innocence.

'When did it happen?'

'It was waiting for us when we got back from our meeting with Marks and Spencer,' says Megan.

'I thought Clive and Connor were on M and S.'

Ralph finally breaks his silence. 'Don't change the subject, Dan. This sort of thing is unacceptable.'

'It's against health and safety,' bleats Megan. 'God knows what deadly microbes it's got in it.'

I can't help laughing. 'Deadly microbes?'

'Google it if you don't believe me.'

'And did *you* google it before or after you sneaked to teacher?'

'I resent that.' Megan looks to Ralph for support, and she gets it.

'My office,' he says to me. 'Five minutes.' He wags his hand vaguely in the direction of the dog shit. 'And clear it up.'

I always carry a couple of bags in my back pocket, and as I crouch down to do the deed, I realise that something's wrong. The thing is, I've come to know Doggo's shit pretty intimately by now, and although it has changed colour and texture over the past couple of weeks, what with more and more people at work slipping him snacks, there has been almost no variation in the essential, underlying consistency of the stuff: dense and on the dry side. The moisture content of the pile in front of me seems unnaturally, suspiciously high.

'What are you waiting for?' asks Megan. Her face is a mask of disgust, but there's also a sort of amused, triumphal glimmer in her eyes.

She didn't! She can't have! She did! But how did she manage to transport it there without damaging it? It's a perfect pile, apparently freshly laid. The answer comes to me as my hand, gloved by the bag, closes around it. It's cold, too cold, not even room temperature.

I'm thrown by Ralph's uncompromising attitude.

'He's going to have to go, I'm afraid.'

'Ralph, it's nothing, a mishap, a one-off. You can't mean it.'

'Megan's adamant.'

'That's not all she is.'

'Careful how you go, Dan.'

Ralph's strange fondness for Megan is rooted in a long history. She was the first creative he recruited at the last agency he set up, and I hold off telling him what I really think: that Doggo's not the issue here, that he's simply a rod for Megan to beat me with, that when it's boiled back to basics, I am the one she doesn't want around.

'It won't happen again.'

'You can't promise that,' says Ralph. 'There's another thing. Technically we're in breach of our lease by having an animal on the premises.'

'It wasn't a problem before.'

'That's because we didn't know before.'

'Don't tell me – Megan pulled the file.'

'It doesn't matter who pulled the file. The landlord's within his rights to throw us out and keep the deposit. Are you happy to pick up the tab for our relocation?'

I've come to know Ralph pretty well – once he's dug his heels in, he's never going to budge – and I'm seriously worried now. 'But he's an asset, good for the office. People love having him around. Even Margaret has changed her tune.'

'I can see that. Which is why it has to happen now, before they get any more attached.'

'Now?'

'End of the week.'

'That's tomorrow.'

'Yes, it is.'

I make my final plea. 'You can't do it to him. He's come to life since being here. It'll destroy him.'

'Dan, get real. He's a dog, he'll be okay.'

But I know he won't be. He'll be devastated, and so will I. He's more than just a pleasing presence in my day, an amusing diversion; he has become part of my personal furniture. I'm tempted to say 'If he goes, I go,' but I'd only be playing into Megan's hands, and I'm not done with her yet, far from it. As for Ralph, I look at him and remember what Tristan told me in confidence at the restaurant the other day, and I think to myself: *You might just have signed your own death warrant, you old bastard.*

Edie grows really quite angry when I tell her. She says she'll get Tristan on to it (which is something she couldn't have said to me a week ago).

'That might not be necessary.'

I spell out my theory about Megan planting the shit in order to frame Doggo.

'My God,' she gasps. 'Turdgate.'

We make a point of working late so that we're the last to leave the creative department. It's Edie's idea to film the search on her phone.

'Action,' she calls.

The bin in the small kitchenette is a flip-top affair. I find what I'm looking for tucked away right down the bottom – a plastic food container. There's only a small amount of residue inside, but the smell of shit is unmistakable. As proof of a crime committed, any defence lawyer worth their salt would tear it to shreds, but it confirms my own suspicions beyond any reasonable doubt: this is the vessel in which Megan transported the frozen dog turd to work. Yes, frozen. That's how she was able to ensure it kept its original shape, its integrity, while in transit. I'm wearing surgical gloves (bought from John Lewis on Oxford Street) when I pull the container from the bin and drop it into the sealable freezer bag (also bought from John Lewis).

'That's a wrap,' says Edie, lowering her phone. I'm not sure if she intended it as a joke until she shoots me a smile. 'Try and keep up.'

The three of us are strolling to Oxford Circus when Edie asks what I'm up to this evening. 'I think we should run through how you intend to play it with Megan tomorrow.'

'It's my football night – six-a-side under the Westway.'

'Are you any good?' she asks.

'Not really.'

'So you won't be missed if I offer to cook you dinner at my place.'

'I'd be surprised if they even noticed.'

Not true. Six versus five is no fun at all, but they'll just have to live with it.

I was wrong about Edie's flat being a stark mecca of minimalist chic. The place looks like it has been burgled. Discarded clothes lie scattered all over, and there are books heaped up in every corner. It turns out that when Douglas decamped, he took most of the storage with him – wardrobe, chest of drawers, sideboard and bookcases. We both know it's a poor excuse for the amount of mess on show. Doggo is in heaven, sniffing and snuffling his way through the clutter. Privately I wonder if he has detected the lurking scent of Tristan.

Edie opens a rather fine bottle of white Burgundy and then shows me how to cook a real risotto alla Milanese.

'Do you always have fresh bone marrow and home-made chicken stock in your fridge?'

'Why, what do you have?'

'Milk. Butter. I eat out a lot.'

'With Doggo?'

'There's a great place up the road with tables outside. They know him now.'

'No social life at all?' she asks with a mischievous grin.

'Yes, actually.'

'Tell me about your friends.'

That's how it starts, and that's how it goes on, me stirring with the wooden spoon while Edie dribbles in the stock with a ladle. She's a good listener, almost too good. There's something evasive about her interest, a sense that the questions are designed to keep me talking about me, about anything but her. Six years is nothing, but it suddenly feels like a lot. At the age of thirty, give or take, most of my friends are up and running in their chosen fields, sure of their choices, forging ahead with their careers. It's Edie who points up the difference. No one she knows has quite broken through, not yet.

'That'll all change when you pick up a D and AD award next year for the SWOSH! campaign.'

'Yeah, right,' she replies sceptically.

'It'll happen one day.'

'How does it feel?'

'Who doesn't want a bit of recognition? It's not like we're working in the charity sector. It feels good.'

She senses my hesitancy. 'But?'

'It's a bauble, a reason for people you don't even know to want you to fail.'

147

'Bugger them.'

I smile. 'That's the spirit. You'll go far.'

'With you, I hope,' she says.

That surprises me. Has she detected my misgivings about the industry we're in? 'I don't see why not.'

'I do,' she replies.

'Oh?'

'Oh?' she parrots perfectly.

'Edie, I have no idea what you're on about.'

She places the ladle on the counter and looks me squarely in the eye. 'Yes you do. He's standing between us. Tell me I'm wrong. Better still, tell me what I have to do.'

I feel suddenly breathless, light-headed. I'm not prepared for this. I've toyed with the thought, but I never for a moment imagined . . .

'End it,' I say.

'End it?'

'Tell him it's over between you.'

The slight clouding in her eyes is the first sign that I've grasped the wrong end of the stick – no, the wrong stick altogether.

'I was talking about Fat Trev,' she says. 'I thought . . .' She trails off. 'I don't know what I thought.'

I do. She fears I'm going to pair up again with my old partner, and I've just gone and completely misinterpreted her words.

The misunderstanding is laughed aside, but the awkwardness lingers like an unpleasant odour in the air around us. Even the distraction of dinner, of the finest risotto I've ever tasted, doesn't dissipate it. Doggo gets his own bowl of the stuff, topped up with extra bone marrow, which he wolfs down before barking for seconds. Edie has a gift for him and she goes rummaging. 'I know it's here somewhere.' She finds it eventually under the sofa: a slender cardboard package from Amazon, unopened.

'What is it?'

'A hunch,' she replies.

It's the DVD of a film called *Marley & Me*, starring Owen Wilson and Jennifer Aniston. The photo on the front shows the two stars trussed up together by a long leash attached to a Golden Labrador puppy. The title rings a vague bell with me, whereas one glimpse of the cover is enough to send Doggo tearing round the room. He makes two frenzied circuits before skidding to a halt and panting up at Edie.

'I thought so,' she says.

Doggo's bizarre obsession with Jennifer Aniston is no longer a mystery. He lies between us on the sofa, chin on his paws, gazing at the TV (when not turning to check we're enjoying the film as much as he is). It's pretty good. Jennifer delivers an impressive performance, and Owen is his utterly watchable and sympathetic self. It's not exactly the laugh-a-minute comedy you might take it to be from the cover. Sure, Marley is an incorrigible handful of a dog, prone to eating furniture and terrorising dog-sitters, but it's really the story of a young couple moving through life, building a family. As for the ending, well, the ending . . .

'Are those tears?' asks Edie as the credits roll.

'Dust mite allergy. What's this sofa stuffed with?'

It's late by now, time to leave. Doggo is presented with the DVD, which he carries off in his mouth when Edie accompanies us downstairs. She crouches and kisses him on the forehead. 'Good night, Doggo. Big day tomorrow.'

'We never talked about Megan and what I'm going to do.'

'Something tells me you'll work it out.'

The timed light in the entrance hall goes off and we find ourselves face to face in the near darkness, just a pale wash of street-lamp sodium slanting through the fanlight above the front door.

'Good night, Dan.'

'Listen, I'm sorry about before.'

'Don't be. I'm not.' She smiles. 'It means I've got something on you too now.'

She certainly does, and I'm not sure I'm ever going to live it down. She lands a quick kiss on my cheek and pulls open the door. 'You should get a cab at the end of the road no problem.'

She's right; we only have to wait a minute or two. Once we're settled on the back seat, Doggo releases the DVD into my charge and rests his head on my lap. There's something wistful in his expression. Maybe I'm wrong, but I sense memories of his former life flapping in to roost.

I run my hand the length of his stumpy little body and make a mental note to call the Battersea Dogs & Cats Home first thing tomorrow.

Chapter Nineteen

I FIGURE THAT MEGAN is less likely to be suspicious if it happens on her own turf, so Edie is drafted in to lure Seth away. She could use pretty much any pretext in the book, given his soft spot for her, but she opts for a game of pool, billing it as an opportunity to avenge herself for her last defeat at his hands.

They're well into their game when I slip silently past them and into the office.

'Hey, Megan. A quick word?'

'About what?' She's at her desk, scribbling away, and only looks up when she hears the door close behind me. 'I've got nothing to say to you.'

I ignore her, pulling up a chair and removing the gaily coloured package from the shopping bag. 'A peace offering.'

'It's not going to do any good.'

'No, I don't suppose it will, but it's yours anyway, so you may as well open it.'

She strips off the wrapping paper to reveal the food container sealed in the freezer bag. Her face falls but recovers quickly.

'Gee, thanks – Tupperware.'

'Second hand, I'm afraid. It's been used to transport dog shit.'

'You really need help.'

'And you really need a lawyer.'

A bit melodramatic, perhaps, but it hits the spot. The supercilious expression falters, and I can almost see her brain at work behind those small, deep-set eyes. She tosses the container at me. 'I've never seen this before.'

'And when your fingerprints are found all over it?' I let my words sink in. 'I used surgical gloves to remove it from the bin. I have video evidence to prove it.'

'What the fuck is this – *CSI: Soho*?'

'You made the rules, I'm just playing by them.'

'Screw you.'

I hesitate before replying. 'You know, Megan, you're a lot of things, but one thing you're not is a figure of fun. When this gets out, you're going to be the laughing stock of the industry. I mean, really . . . framing a dog with a frozen turd?'

She's impressively quick on her feet. 'Come to think of it, when I found the turd, I cleared it away in my Tupperware there. But then I thought: no way, I want people to see what that bloody dog has done, so I put it back and threw the Tupperware away.'

'Not bad, as lies go.'

'You know it. I know it. No one else will.'

'Thanks, that's all I needed to hear.' I slip the container into the shopping bag and rise to my feet. 'Oh, I guess you should know . . .'

I pull back the cuff of my shirt to reveal the tiny microphone taped to my wrist. It cost me £60 from Spymaster on Portman Square. The digital recording device in my pocket was a further £120. I'd happily have spent ten times that much to clear Doggo's name.

There's pure venom in Megan's voice when she finally finds it. 'That's lower than low.'

'Are you seriously going to lecture me about playing dirty?' I turn at the door. 'If you want to talk more, I'll be in my office.'

Ralph describes it as a stay of execution. It seems Megan has had a change of heart. 'She doesn't want to press charges, so to speak.'

'Oh?'

'She says she rather likes having Doggo around.'

'Oh?'

Ralph plants his elbows on his desk, scrutinising me. 'What did you do, Dan? Was it money? Did you buy her off?'

'I don't know what you mean.'

He gives a sceptical grunt. 'There's still the issue of that clause in our tenancy agreement.'

'He's a mental health companion dog. I don't imagine that's a deal-breaker when it comes to the lease.'

Ralph throws his head back and laughs. 'You're a dark horse. I can see I'm going to have to keep my eye on you.'

'It's not me you need to worry about.'

That sobers him up pretty quickly. Me too. I wasn't planning to say it.

'Go on,' he says.

★

Edie thinks we should celebrate Doggo's deliverance in style, so after work we stroll through Covent Garden to the bar overlooking the river at Somerset House. We nab some comfy armchairs on the terrace, where Edie orders two glasses of champagne for us and a plate of dried meats for Doggo. She asks to hear the recording I made of my conversation with Megan. Playing it back, I'm struck by how hard I sound, how pitiless. Is that really my voice, really me?

'Wow, you stitched her up nice and tight.'

I don't tell her how I then went and did the same thing to Tristan.

Ralph fell into a brooding silence when I told him what Tristan had implied to me at the restaurant: that before too long he, Ralph, would not be in a position to call the shots at Indology.

'That little shit,' he finally muttered. 'Thanks, Dan, I owe you.'

I can't trust Ralph to keep me out of it, despite his promise to. He's the sort of man who's likely to let something slip in the heat of the moment. And Tristan's no fool, he'll suspect my involvement. I'm still not sure why I did it. I think maybe my blood was running high with virtuous indignation after the confrontation with Megan. Whatever the reason, I've started a war, and everyone knows that once that particular genie is out of the bottle there's really no putting it back.

'To Doggo,' says Edie. 'Long may he deliver letters.' We raise our champagne flutes to him, and I could swear there's something in the set of his lips that suggests a smile.

I've spent almost twenty-four hours squirming at the memory of my unwitting confession to Edie, whereas she seems to have taken it in her stride. It's as though it never happened, which I guess is the message she's sending me: it didn't, let's both move on. There's just one problem – I'm not sure I want to move on, not if it means going back to where we were.

'Listen, I never got a chance to say last night, but you don't have to worry about Fat Trev and me. That's over, gone for good.'

'Really?'

I fill her in on my awkward dinner with Trev the other evening. 'He blames the job for sending him over the edge. He's not coming back.'

'What if he changes his mind?'

'I've made my choice too, and it's you.'

With a sudden lurch of the stomach, I realise how that must sound to her. 'Oh God, I didn't mean it like that.'

'But you did last night,' she replies teasingly.

'That's not fair. I was drunk.'

'You'd had one glass of wine. We were making risotto.'

'Yeah, well, making risotto does strange things to me. It always has.'

She has a dinner later, and so do I – J and Lily's first since they got back together. It'll be one of their big Friday night feasts with loads of people jammed in around the giant refectory table in the kitchen. I also have an appointment at the dogs home tomorrow morning to see if I can extract some more information about Doggo. When Edie hears this, she asks if I want company.

'Sure, if you're free at eleven thirty.'

'Free all day,' she replies, which may or may not be an invitation to spend it with her. We'll see.

★

J has always been the king of cocktails. It's more than an art for him, it's alchemy, which is why he calls his own lethal concoction 'The Philosopher's Stone' (or 'La Pietra Filosofale', seeing as it was invented in Italy during his gap year before university). The contents are a closely guarded secret that he has vowed only to reveal to his first-born child. This means it has to be prepared in strict privacy and in advance, usually in a large silver bowl, so technically it's not a cocktail but a punch − a far more fitting moniker. The first glass is like a slap in the face with a wet fish. The second, bizarrely, is like a gentle caress. That's the one I'm on when J claps his hands together, calling the rowdy mob in the back garden to order.

'I have an announcement to make.' He glances at Lily, who's standing beside him. '*We* have an announcement to make.' There's a low murmur of anticipation; we're all thinking the same thing. 'It's no secret that Lily and I have had our wobbles over the years. Well, you can't learn to ride a bike without a few wobbles, and that's what I want to talk about.' Lily's eyes roll heavenwards in weary forbearance. 'A bike,' says J. 'One of you lot has chained theirs to the neighbours' railings and they're threatening to call the cops and have it removed.'

A collective groan goes up. J ducks to avoid a cocktail sausage, which Doggo snaffles up, and Lily has the last laugh. 'Come on, guys, you really think I would have said yes?'

Lily is a serious cook with an ambitious and varied repertoire. Tonight she has gone Moroccan. We're treated to a variety of exotic appetisers and home-made flatbreads before the tagines, couscous and salads hit the table. J has managed to find a very drinkable Moroccan red wine (as well as a watery white that isn't in the same league). It's a hard combination to beat: great food and good friends. I realise I'm the only person at the table who isn't paired off right now, although a couple of the partners are missing, away on business.

I've lain low over the past month or so and it's inevitable I'm going to be quizzed about Clara. When I am, I come clean about Wayne, the budding movie-maker from New Zealand. The news rips round the table. 'Dan, you poor thing.' 'Why didn't you say?' 'I can't believe it.' 'I can,' says J. I want to tell them I'm okay with it, that Clara hardly figures in my thoughts any more, but they'll only think I'm putting on a brave face, so I field the questions, make the right noises, and the talk finally, thankfully, turns to other things.

I know I'm going to be the last to leave, although Charlie and Anna give me a run for my money. We're well into the whisky by the time they finally stagger off. J and I blitz the washing-up while Lily plays DJ and tries to get Doggo interested in a tennis ball.

'He doesn't do balls,' I explain.

'First dog I've met that doesn't.'

'He's in love with Jennifer Aniston.'

J shakes his head despairingly. 'I've got to say it, mate—'

Lily cuts him off. 'No you don't.'

J ignores her. 'This whole one-man-and-his-dog thing . . . it's kind of creepy. You couldn't stand the bloody thing when Clara first showed up with it, and now that she's buggered off, you're all over it.'

'J, shut up,' says Lily.

'I mean, what are you doing? Holding it for her till she returns?'

'He's not hers any more, he's mine.'

J turns to Lily. 'See what I mean?' He hands me a salad bowl to dry. 'And another thing, he's not going to do you any favours when it comes to attracting the ladies. Maybe if he was a black Lab or something.'

I know that look in Doggo's eye; it's the same one he has when he's gazing at Megan. 'Watch how you go. You're about to make yourself an enemy.'

'Jesus . . .' mutters J.

'Don't bother, Doggo, he's not worth it.' I squat down beside him and scratch his snout. 'And I know a girl who finds you just as handsome as I do.'

'Mate, she's lying.'

'Who?' asks Lily, her interest piqued. 'Come on, out with it.'

I tell them about Edie. I tell them almost everything. It's the reason I've hung around.

'Doggo,' says Lily, 'I think your master's falling in love.'

'No I'm not.'

'Pants on fire.'

'Well, maybe a little.'

J is a simple soul at heart – he has no trouble grasping base impulses like physical desire – so the moment he sees the photo of Edie on my phone I have his full blessing. 'Knockout,' he says. 'Top drawer. Go for it.'

'I think I might already have blown it.'

I now tell them the rest – my faux pas the other night, Tristan, everything. I need guidance, advice. I listen and watch as they sweetly attempt to agree on something for once. J is firmly of the view that women have to be fought for tooth and nail, even carried off by force if the situation requires it.

'It's not the rape of the bloody Sabines,' says Lily. She turns to me. 'Ignore him, Dan. Just be yourself.'

'Like *that's* going to work,' snorts J.

I know he's only half joking.

Chapter Twenty

I ONLY REALISE MY mistake when the three of us are shown into Beth's office at the Battersea Dogs & Cats Home.

'He still hasn't been dealt with, I see.'

I should have left Doggo behind, or at least outside with Edie. 'It's in the pipeline,' I say. Beth looks unconvinced. 'Life's been pretty crazy since I was last here. I started a new job. In fact, so has Doggo.'

I assume she'll find it endearing to hear that he has become the office postman.

'He's even started tweeting,' chips in Edie. It's true. Anna on reception has set him up with an account.

It's hard to decipher the look in Beth's eye as she peers at Doggo, but I'd say it's not so much one of affection as of sympathy – compassion of the kind you'd feel for an exploited child labourer in an Asian sweatshop. 'Well, he doesn't look too bad on it,' she concedes grudgingly.

I kept it vague when I made the appointment because it's information I'm after, and what organisation hands that out freely in this data-protection-obsessed age of ours? Better to spring it on Beth in person, I figured, winning it out of her with charm. Unfortunately, everything about Beth suggests she doesn't recall our last meeting with the same fondness I do.

She listens impassively as I fill her in on Doggo's fascination with Jennifer Aniston, and how it set me thinking about his former life, where he came from. 'I mean, I know he wasn't abandoned, but that's about it.'

Beth has the file in front of her. 'No, that's right, he wasn't. His owner brought him in.'

'I'd love to have a word with them, you know, fill in some of the gaps, maybe get some tips – what he likes, that sort of thing. Who knows, maybe they'd like to follow him on Twitter, stay in touch that way.'

Beth closes the file and immediately gives away the sex of the previous owner. 'I don't know why he brought Doggo in. Despite what you may think, we don't interrogate people.' She says it with a wounded note in her voice, which is when I remember that I made an unwise reference to Nazis last time I was here. That's obviously why she's being so frosty. 'Maybe he couldn't cope with a dog any more,' she continues. 'Maybe it was money. It can be a big wrench for the owners too, saying goodbye. We see our fair share of tears. I'm not sure he'd want to be reminded of it.'

'But he might,' says Edie.

'I can't give out personal details even if I wanted to. We have a strict privacy policy. I'm sure you understand.'

'And is forwarding a letter out of the question?' I ask.

Beth thinks on it for a moment. 'No, that might be possible . . . if you're happy to keep your side of the bargain.' Her eyes flick in Doggo's direction. Am I wrong? The message seems to be: get him castrated and I'll consider it. It's a good thing that Edie's the first of us to find her voice.

'That's great. Thank you. Like Dan said, it's in the pipeline.' She smiles sweetly at me with eyes that order: just be a good boy.

'Absolutely. Thanks, Beth.'

I only know for sure that Edie's up to something when she announces that she's dead set on getting a dog too. Beth perks up, happy to do the honours. We're all heading downstairs when I get a text from Edie: *Phone me on my signal*

The kennel block is a cacophony of barks and yelps, with the odd strangled howl thrown in. Maybe Doggo has blanked the memory of his brief stay here; he seems more intrigued than disturbed by the tall cells flanking the corridor, with their barred doors and their agitated occupants. The dogs come in all shapes and sizes, and we've already visited a fair few of them when Edie tips me the wink. I surreptitiously call her mobile, then watch in wonderment as she goes to work.

'Mum, hi . . . Not the best time, I'm in the middle of something. Can it wait? . . . Of course I care. How's he doing? . . . Hold on a second.' She presses the phone to her chest and turns to us, her face furrowed with apology. 'I'm sorry but I've really got to take this.' She rolls her eyes for Beth's benefit and whispers the word 'mothers', before sidling off. 'Let me find somewhere quieter . . . Dogs . . . Yes, dogs. I'll explain later. Tell me how he is . . .'

Her performance is so convincing that as soon as she's lost to view, I find myself saying to Beth, 'Her grandad had a fall the other day.'

★

It's as I guessed: Edie was after Doggo's file. Beth left it out on her desk and we now have a name – Patrick Ellory – along with a mobile number. What exactly to do with them requires a bit of thought, and we still haven't settled on a strategy by the time we've strolled through Battersea Park and over Albert Bridge. We find ourselves a table in the sun among the toytown shacks of Chelsea Farmers Market.

'You should have been an actor.'

'I wanted to be,' she replies. 'I tried for the National Youth Theatre in my last year at school. They said no.'

'More fool them. I'm not sure I'm ever going to believe another word you say.'

'More fool you. That was complete bullshit.'

'Really?'

She smiles. 'No, I tried, didn't make the cut. I was okay, competent, but I could never really let go, lose myself.' She sneaks a sip of her beer. 'It's the same with my relationships, at least that's what my boyfriends have always told me.'

I don't want to talk about Tristan. 'Three years with Douglas, you must have done something right.'

'Two years too long. That's what he said, not me, but he was right. It just took me a while to realise it.'

I've always assumed that Douglas was dumped in favour of Tristan, but it seems the relationship just petered out by mutual consent. 'We were more like brother and sister at the end. There were no hard feelings, even when he shacked up with my best friend.'

Our dilemma is this (and pleasingly it *has* become our dilemma now, not just mine): we can't be honest with Patrick Ellory. If we are, he's liable to react badly, shut us out, even lodge a complaint with the dogs home. Edie thinks she should phone him up pretending to be from Battersea and say that the new owner of Mikey (I still can't get over that name) is keen to get in touch. If Ellory agrees, I'm free to phone him. If he doesn't, we're stymied.

Edie makes the call but hangs up when it goes to message. She'll try again in a bit.

'What does he sound like?'

'Well-spoken. Friendly. Oldish.'

I'm struck by a sudden thought. Doggo is curled at our feet in the shade under the table. 'Where's Patrick?' I ask. He raises a lazy eye towards me, apparently unmoved by the name. 'Patrick!' Still nothing, not even the slightest glimmer of recognition.

'That's weird for a dog so good with names,' says Edie.

She suggests we head to the South Kensington branch of Christie's, a short walk away, to see which auctions are viewing. 'It worked for us last time.' It certainly did. The breakthrough on the strapline for SWOSH! came as we wandered back to the office after viewing the Impressionist & Modern sale.

Vintage Posters isn't quite in the same league, although many of the lots on show in the ground-floor galleries are French, as is the Vargo, the new hatchback we're still struggling to find an angle on. We're not the only ones. Clive and Connor claim to have hit a wall, unless the furious rows (worse than ever) have been staged to deceive.

Ralph knew exactly what he was doing when he threw the brief open to the whole creative department. For all his talk of pulling together, he was pitting us against each other. It's pretty clear that whichever team impresses him the most on

Wednesday will get the job. Megan is playing her cards very close and has obviously sworn Seth to silence. I wouldn't be surprised if we're all coming at it the same way, though, focusing on the goodies wrapped up in the ugly package: the great fuel economy and the cool kit that comes as standard (including satnav and hands-free Bluetooth connectivity). There's no denying you get a lot of bang for your buck; unfortunately there's an eye-watering price to be paid in the looks department.

Edie and I get a boost of inspiration from some of the old posters, with their stylised images of long-forgotten French liqueurs, razor-bowed ocean liners, speeding locomotives and palm-fringed spa resorts on the Riviera. There's only one problem: they are all testaments to the seductive power of style over substance, whereas substance is the only card we can logically play when it comes to promoting the decidedly un-seductive, style-free Vargo.

Edie is the one to point out this unfortunate disparity. Once she has, the easy elegance of the posters begins to taunt us from the walls. It's time to move on, anyway; Edie has a hair appointment in Marylebone.

I don't know any women who wear their hair as short as she does. 'Just a trim, I suppose.'

'Depends,' she replies. 'How short do you think I should go?'

'Ripley in *Alien 3*. You could get away with it.'

'I might just do that.'

Doggo and I see her to South Kensington tube, where she tries Patrick Ellory's number once again, and again it goes to message. She promises to call me as soon as she has spoken to him. Almost as an afterthought, she mentions that she's meeting up for lunch tomorrow with some friends at a riverside pub out near Richmond. Annoyingly, I can't join them; it would mean blowing out lunch with my mother, who's over from Spain for Pat Connelly's funeral.

'Why didn't you say?'

'I think I might have overreacted to what Grandpa said.'

I can tell she thinks I'm trying to make light of it, but I'm really not. When Mum called on Thursday to fix a time and a place to meet, there was nothing in her voice to suggest she would be sharing anything more sinister with me tomorrow than a Sunday roast.

Chapter Twenty-One

M Y MOTHER IS manically punctual. I know this, which is why I make a special effort to turn up on time, which is why I'm not as late as I usually am. Twelve minutes is about as good as it gets. It's also time enough for Mum to sink most of her Bloody Mary, I note.

The drink has taken the edge off her sulk. She doesn't want to be eating here, but the restaurant she and Nigel favour, the one just down the road from the hotel they always stay at when in London, doesn't accept dogs.

'He's better in the flesh,' is the most she can offer when she sets eyes on Doggo.

'You can stroke him if you want.'

'Do I have to, darling?'

'He's safe. I've treated him for fleas. And worms.'

'You did that? All by yourself?' She sounds pleasantly surprised and even gives Doggo a couple of awkward pats on the head.

'Where's Nigel?' I ask.

It's a poor excuse, something to do with a last-minute business meeting he couldn't get out of, and it sets me wondering, thinking things I don't want to be thinking. They're soon forgotten in a flurry of chatter about Pat Connelly's funeral tomorrow and the many ghosts from the past Mum is expecting (and mostly dreading) to see at the crematorium out in Hertfordshire.

'Is Dad going to be there?'

'I don't know. I don't suppose so. Pat was one of the few friends who took my side when he left me for the lesbian.'

'Mum, I don't think Carol's a lesbian.'

'Darling, don't be so naive. They're just as good at hiding themselves as the queers.'

At moments like this, the generation gap seems more like an unbridgeable chasm. 'No one says queers any more.'

'Then you pick the word. I think I'm going to start with the oysters.'

Mum has always liked a glass of wine – the pop of a cork at six o'clock is an abiding childhood memory of mine – but she throws back the Saint-Véran like she's trying to put out a fire. When I tell her to slow down, she tells me she's trying to. It's a cryptic response, and the first real sign of what's coming. I only have to wait a couple of seconds for the next, and there's nothing cryptic about this one.

'I lied to you about Grandpa.' She just blurts it out.

'About Grandpa?'

'You know what I mean.'

'Help me out.'

'About what he said to you.' She can't hold my gaze. 'Oh God. Bloody Nigel.'

'Nigel?'

'He said you had a right to know the truth. But he's wrong.

Nothing good can come of it and now it's too late . . .' She dabs at the welling tears with her napkin.

I feel numb yet remarkably alert, like I've been plunged into an icy lake. I reach blindly for Doggo down by my feet and find comfort in the rasp of his tongue against the back of my hand. Even if I could think of something to say, I'm not sure I could produce the words. I can see that Mum is struggling too.

'I'm sorry, sweetpea,' she finally manages to choke out.

'Who?' I ask.

'I can't say. Not yet. You see, he doesn't know.'

'Doesn't know?'

'That you're his. I have to talk to him first.' She shakes her head in self-reprimand. 'I should have talked to him first. That was the idea, but looking at you there . . . well, it just came out.'

'Mum, you're going to have to give me more than that.'

She does, quietly and with a controlled dignity that's at odds with the scandalous story she tells. It seems the University of East Anglia campus was a hotbed of sexual promiscuity during the late seventies and early eighties. I'm surprised to hear that Dad (Dad?), for all his high-minded posturing, munched freely on the forbidden fruit, which in his case usually took the form of besotted female students. Mum was expected to tolerate his many trysts – sexual possession was a bourgeois construct, don't you know – and even indulge in some of her own. She tried it a couple of times before Emma was born, but unwillingly, almost dutifully, hoping to stir in Dad (that word again) some last vestige of decency or jealousy. Then, after Emma was born, she tried it again, not because she thought she should this time, but because she wanted to.

'He was very special. Young. Gentle. Very handsome. And so funny.'

I can see the tendrils of memory drawing her off to another place. 'Mum,' I say, to bring her back.

'You have the same profile. Men with strong profiles are rarely found wanting. Who said that?'

'I don't know. How young?'

'He was studying for his PhD in the Climate Research Unit.'

'He's a scientist?'

'Not any more, maybe on the side, I don't know. He's made a name for himself in a completely different field.'

'Good name or bad name?'

'That depends on your politics.'

UEA in 1982? He had to be left-wing, probably New Labour. 'Oh God, I'm Tony Blair's love child.'

She laughs. 'No.'

'Who?'

'I told you, I can't say, not till I've spoken to him. You've waited long enough, a little while longer won't hurt.'

My anger rises suddenly and unexpectedly to the surface. 'There's a difference between waiting and being kept in the total bloody dark for thirty years.'

I'm vaguely aware of the couple at the neighbouring table reacting to my raised voice, and of Mum reaching for my hand. 'You're right about one thing,' she says softly. 'You *were* a love child. I knew exactly what I was doing. You weren't a mistake. It was reckless – God, it was reckless – but I wanted to make a baby with him. I know he wanted the same. He wanted me to leave your father . . . leave Michael.'

'So why didn't you?'

She hesitates, searching for the answer in her wine glass. 'I don't know. I was scared, I suppose, scared that it would hold him back. He was just a boy, but clearly going places. And there was Emma, too. Don't forget Emma. We were a family.'

'She has no idea?'

'No one does.'

'Except Grandpa. And bloody Nigel.'

She stiffens in her chair. 'Bloody Nigel is the reason we're having this discussion, so it would be nice if you showed him a little more respect. I know he's not your type, but he's a good man, and there aren't too many of those around, take it from me.'

I hang my head. 'I'm sorry.'

'You're forgiven. *I* don't expect to be. Not yet. Maybe someday.'

I know I'm in shock, not thinking straight, but I'm pretty sure I've never heard my mother speak like this, with such feeling, such searing honesty. She even looks different. It's as if the lie has lain over her like a veil all these years and only now can I see her as she really is.

All okay. Nothing to report. Feel like a total arse.

That's the basic thrust of the text I promised to send Edie. I can't face telling her the truth. She'll want to talk it through, maybe even meet up after her lunch out in Richmond, whereas I just want to walk, feel the ground beneath my feet, because that at least is solid, reliable.

Edie's reply lands in my phone as Doggo and I are entering Hyde Park at Speakers' Corner: *That's good, but bad for my mother who was hoping for more! X*

I can't think of anything to say in return, so I listen instead – to the usual smattering of religious nuts and other harmless crackpots holding forth from their soapboxes and stepladders. Is it really possible that JFK was assassinated because he was about to reveal the truth about the Roswell UFO crash? The evidence is a little patchy. The best of the bunch is a young man, surprisingly articulate, who claims to have it on good authority that Simon Cowell has recently been elevated to the ranks of the New World Order, the sinister cabal of Freemasons, Illuminati, Jews, Jesuits, bankers and other undesirables who for centuries have been running world affairs from the shadows. He somehow manages to work 9/11 and global warming into the mix.

There's something invigorating about this cat's cradle of conspiracy theories. To the truly paranoid, anything is possible. Better still, my own story, the one just sprung on me, seems dull and commonplace by comparison.

Doggo and I are skirting the Serpentine when I'm taken by a sudden urge to lie down. Spread-eagled on my back in the shade of a large oak, I search for meaningful patterns in the canopy of boughs and branches. Doggo nudges me with his snout and bounces around. This is a first. Does he really want me to play with him? Maybe he senses my black mood and is trying to shake me out of it. If so, he doesn't succeed.

'Excuse me. Is that your dog?'

The words don't mean anything, not at first, not until I wake to see a woman with long auburn hair staring down at me. She doesn't look happy. I force myself into a sitting position. 'Sorry?'

She points. 'That dog, is he yours? He's stolen our ball.'

I see two young girls standing with a Welsh terrier, and a man (presumably the girls' father) edging closer to Doggo, who does indeed have a tennis ball in his mouth.

'There's a good dog now, drop it, drop the ball.' Doggo darts off out of range. 'Bloody mongrel!'

I let the insult go – just. 'Don't worry, I'll get it back.'

Famous last words. I finally persuade Doggo to release the ball, but as I reach for it, he suddenly snatches it up again and shoots between my legs. The man lunges, misses, ends up on his knees. 'Doggo!' I yell, chasing after him.

He gives us the runaround for a good few minutes before he finally relinquishes his prize. My apologies fall on deaf ears.

'You should learn to control him,' says the man.

I turn to his daughters. 'Was that fun?'

'Yes,' they chime in unison, delighted to have watched two grown men brought low by a small dog.

I hand the man the moist tennis ball. 'Not a total waste of time, then.'

Doggo only approaches me once they've moved on. He steps carefully, cautiously, but when I drop to my knees, he hurries forward and allows himself to be swept off his feet.

'It's okay, I'm back now. Thank you, you sweet thing.'

He licks my face and I blow a raspberry into his neck.

Chapter Twenty-Two

THE CARTOON IS waiting for me on my desk when I show up for work on Monday morning, along with a note from Josh: *Had another bash at it over the weekend.*

I have to laugh. He has stuck with the same three frames – M-m-m-m . . . D-d-d-d . . . McDonald's! – but he has added a dog at the table, a dog clearly modelled on Doggo! He has also tweaked the expressions of the parents so that it's now the dog's reaction that draws the eye. There's something brilliantly world-weary in its look of incredulity when the baby blurts out 'McDonald's'. It's a stroke of genius; the gag still works, but the dog has now become the story. You're left with a sense that the poor wise creature has been lumbered with this modish young couple (the father's designer spectacles are another great addition) for whom life will never quite go as planned.

Edie loves it. Tristan claims to. He seems a little out of sorts, and when he collars me at the coffee machine, I understand why.

'Good weekend?' he asks.

'Not bad. You?'

'What did you get up to?'

He's not the sort to make small talk about my weekend; he clearly knows and is trying to catch me out. I fill him in on our expedition to the dogs home.

'Whose idea was it?' he demands.

'Mine.'

'Edie says it was hers.'

'It was my idea to go. She asked if she could tag along. Tristan, why are we even having this conversation?'

He edges closer, invading my space. 'I just want to know we're singing from the same hymn sheet.' He's so sure of himself, so convinced of his ability to intimidate me.

'Hey,' I say, 'I'm your wing man.'

He likes that – the craven reply, the knowing nod to *Top Gun* – and he lays a hand on my shoulder, anointing me with his forgiveness. 'Okay. Just checking.'

There were a couple of times over the weekend when I doubted my decision to tip Ralph the wink about Tristan. I have no regrets now. I hope the cogs are turning and he's headed for a fall. Edie claims to know another side to him, and maybe it's there somewhere, but the truth is, I think less of her because of him.

I don't put it quite like that to her; I tell her she's going to have to start filling me in on what she has and hasn't told him. 'That's twice now he's warned me off you.'

'Twice?'

'I didn't say before. My lunch with him was the first time.'

She seems amused by the thought. 'What did he say?'

'You really want to know?'

'I do.'

'If you fuck her, I'll fire you.'

'He said that?'

'Poetic, huh?'

She swivels in her desk chair to face me. 'Dan, I'm not responsible for his neuroses.'

'I just want to be left alone. I don't want him shoving his face in mine while I'm making a coffee. Is that too much to ask?'

'No.'

'It's probably best if we don't socialise any more.'

'Okay,' she replies.

'Strictly professional.'

'I can do strictly professional.'

'Good.'

Despite Doggo's best efforts, I've been wound tight as a drum since my lunch with Mum yesterday, and Edie isn't the first to feel the sting of my irritability. When I offered up my seat on the bus this morning, I was rewarded with a sneer and a question: 'Why, because I'm a woman?'

'No, because I'm a gentleman. But if you're happy standing, that's just fine by us, isn't it, Doggo?'

He gave a little yap by way of reply.

'I won't tell you what he said.'

This drew some satisfying chuckles from our fellow passengers.

The call from Patrick Ellory comes just after lunch. I know it's him because Edie suddenly morphs into Annabelle Theakston from Battersea Dogs & Cats Home. The gist of their conversation is this: Ellory has only just spotted the missed calls on his mobile because he was abroad until this morning; and he's more than happy to talk to Mikey's new owner, although Mikey was his aunt's dog so he's not sure how helpful he'll be. Wisely, Edie keeps it simple, curbing her curiosity; Annabelle Theakston would surely have all these details, and possibly more, at her fingertips.

She scribbles down Ellory's number. 'Over to you,' she says, handing me the Post-it, and I can tell from her tone that she's still smarting from our frosty exchange earlier.

'Not now. Later.'

'Don't mention it,' she says pointedly.

'I'm sorry. Thanks. You were scarily convincing again.'

She shrugs. 'Maybe I'm wrong, but I got the feeling the aunt is dead.' She has lowered her voice for Doggo's benefit, and we both now glance at him on his sofa.

Later, at home, I research dogs and grief on the Internet. The most graphic evidence that our four-legged friends can feel a very real sense of loss is a video I find on YouTube of a Siberian husky sobbing like a human on the grave of its dead mistress. Maybe Doggo was denied even that, it occurs to me. The sight of the gravestone serves as a reminder to call my mother.

Nigel picks up in their hotel room.

'Hi, Nigel, it's me.'

'Daniel,' he replies guardedly.

'Listen, thanks for persuading Mum to come clean with me.'

'Really?'

'Really. I appreciate it.'

'*De nada, amigo.*'

When Mum comes on the line, I ask her how the funeral went today.

'Have you ever been to a crematorium? Poor Pat. It was

ghastly. A factory. In and out. Barely time to change the music. Some people scatter the ashes in the memorial garden. Ashes!? I saw bits of bone in the rose borders!' She asks me how I'm feeling.

'Oh, you know – the wrong side of confused.'

'Of course you are. I was right to tell you, wasn't I?'

'Yes, I think so.'

'You don't sound convinced.'

'What if he doesn't want to meet me?'

'It's possible. I'd be surprised, though.'

She'd be surprised, but I'd be left in some weird limbo, caught between two fathers, effectively ignored by the one who thinks he sired me and rejected by the other, who did. I can't bank on a happy reunion after thirty years. I know from Mum that he has a family of his own, a wife, children, and I really wouldn't want to do anything to jeopardise that. After all, he's as much a victim of this situation as I am. Until yesterday, neither of us even knew the other existed; we were united in our ignorance. Mum didn't exactly set out to trick him, but as she said, she knew what she was doing, allowing herself to fall pregnant by him. He has every right to take the news badly.

'It's sweet of you to think of it from his side,' says Mum. 'But then you always were a considerate boy.'

Or maybe I'm just preparing myself for the worst. Mum has established that he's on holiday right now, and even when he gets back she's going to have to play the situation very carefully, diplomatically, out of respect for his circumstances. It'll help her cause that I'm not looking to rock any boats. I've told her I don't want or need any kind of public recognition from him (or even a clandestine relationship, for that matter). All I'm asking for is a chance to sit down and look my biological father in the eye. I've also decided that no one else needs to know, not Dad, not Emma.

'Really, Danny? Are you sure?' The surprise in Mum's voice is coupled with a palpable note of relief.

'What's the point?'

'Honesty?' she suggests tentatively.

'Christ, at what price? I can't face the fallout. Can you?'

'It's your decision.'

'Yes, it is. And thanks for letting me get there by myself.'

I hear her stifle a sudden loud sob. 'Oh God . . .'

'What?'

'How did you get to be so . . . so grounded?'

'Clara calls it cold-hearted.'

'That girl's a fool. One day she'll wake up and realise what she's done.'

Chapter Twenty-Three

'YOU STILL HAVEN'T called him?' asks Edie.

'The evening sort of ran away with me. Suddenly it was too late.'

It's a version of the truth. By 9.30 p.m., after my long conversation with Mum, I'd sunk the best part of a bottle of Rioja and couldn't face slurring my way through a conversation with Patrick Ellory.

'Do it now,' says Edie. 'I insist.'

'Oh, you do, do you?'

'Come on, Doggo, let's give Mr Hopeless some privacy.'

He answers his phone with just one word – 'Ellory' – but it's loaded with warmth and jocularity. I see an Englishman in the traditional mould, good at sports and fixing things. He's a barrister, due in court later, but more than happy to chat away about his Aunt Geraldine, Doggo's former owner. 'Nutty as a fruit cake. Always was. Never found anyone clever enough or stupid enough to marry her.'

She spent her whole life in the same house in Wandsworth, a large double-fronted property with a wild expanse of garden, which is where she discovered Doggo, cowering in the old

Anderson shelter beside the potting shed (just as she had done as a young girl during the Blitz).

'She'd been feeding him up for a couple of weeks when I first met him and he still looked like he was at death's door. God only knows what state he was in when she found him. My wife called them "the odd couple", and they were, knocking around that crazy old house together. You know, I think he was the husband she never had, the only living thing she ever really loved. I'm glad for her she found that happiness at the end. Are you still there?'

'Yes, I'm sorry, this is very interesting. What happened to her?'

'She had a massive stroke.'

Doggo was the one who alerted the neighbours. When the ambulance arrived, they had to break into the place because all the doors and windows were locked, or so it first appeared. They later found that one of the dormer windows in the roof was open, which meant that Doggo had made his way up there and outside on to the slates.

'I've seen it and it's one hell of a drop, even with the rhododendron bush I'm guessing he landed in. He must have. There's no other way he could have survived that fall.'

Ellory still feels bad about dumping Doggo at Battersea, but it wasn't feasible to integrate him into their life, already ruled by a couple of cats. 'And none of my cousins wanted him. They're more concerned about putting the house on the market and cashing in. But I'm the one with power of attorney over her estate, and I'd never let that happen as long as she's alive.'

'Excuse me?'

'It's the principle of the thing.'

'No, I mean . . . she's alive?'

'Didn't I say?'

'She's alive!?' says Edie.

'After a fashion. I think the phrase he used was "persistent vegetative state".'

'But she's alive.'

'Technically, I suppose.'

She casts a glance at Doggo. 'You know what we have to do, don't you?'

'No.'

'Liar.'

'Edie, we can't. She's a vegetable. Is that how you want him to remember her?'

She grabs my forearm. 'Dan, I have a feeling about this. Trust me. We have to do it.'

I know she's won, but I'm not going down without a fight. 'I thought we said no socialising.'

'This is work.' She flashes me a smile. 'We're talking about the office postman, remember?'

St George's Hospital in Tooting is a vast, sprawling complex of impressively unattractive brick buildings (conveniently located, I notice, just across the road from Lambeth Cemetery).

I hang back with Doggo while Edie makes a first foray inside. We've figured that they're not going to let us just waltz into the stroke unit with a dog at ours heels, and we're right. Edie returns with the news that guide dogs only (and in special circumstances) is their hard-and-fast policy on animals. 'I was tempted to ask about the ones they're butchering right now in the name of medical research.'

'I didn't know you were an animal rights activist.'

'You should have seen me at university. I had a balaclava and everything.'

It's a simple plan. We'll smuggle Doggo inside in my backpack. There's only one problem: he won't go anywhere near it, let alone climb inside it. The more we try and coax him, the more mistrustful he becomes. He even growls and gives me a warning nip on the hand. I tell him we're going to find Geraldine; I tell him Geraldine is desperate to see him; I tell him Geraldine has a giant bag of Choc Drops waiting for him. He won't be swayed.

'Maybe he's claustrophobic,' suggests Edie.

No, there's something else. He'll jump off a roof for her, but climbing into a backpack is a step too far? It doesn't make sense. I pull out my phone and call Patrick Ellory. It goes to message. 'Patrick, it's Daniel here. I'm sorry to bother you again, but I'm just wondering if Mikey knew Geraldine by another name.'

We stroll the streets for a bit before installing ourselves in the beer garden of a dismal pub. An hour later, we're still there and even Edie's enthusiasm is beginning to flag. Reluctantly she agrees to call it a day. The three of us are making for Tooting Broadway tube station when Patrick Ellory calls back: 'You're absolutely right. She was always Zsa Zsa to him.'

'Like the actress?'

'*Moulin Rouge* was her favourite film.'

I wait till we're back in the hospital car park before springing it on Doggo. 'Where's Zsa Zsa?' He visibly stiffens, his eyes searching mine for signs that we're talking about the same thing. 'Let's go and see Zsa Zsa.' He barks three times and spins on the spot like a dervish. I squat beside him with the backpack and he jams himself inside it head first. I manoeuvre him round the other way and raise my finger to my lips. 'Shhh,' I say as I close the zip on his wide-eyed and expectant little face.

We're taking the lift to the second floor of the Atkinson Morley Wing when I see that it's just gone 8 p.m. – the cut-off point for visiting.

'Relax,' says Edie. 'Just let me do the talking.'

No amount of talking will blag us to Geraldine's bedside in the stroke unit, because she has been moved to the intensive care unit. When we get there, Edie tells me to wait outside. I'm talking to Doggo over my shoulder, assuring him it won't be long now, which is why I don't see the two hospital porters approaching along the corridor until they're almost level with me. I smile and nod at them. 'Evening,' I say, and from the look they exchange, they evidently think I'm on the lam from the psychiatric unit.

Edie reappears. 'Okay, here it is – she's my grandmother, you're my boyfriend, and we've just flown in from Vancouver.'

'What were we doing in Vancouver?'

'God knows. I didn't say. It just came to me.'

'Maybe it's where we live.'

'If you want.'

'I hear it's a great place – right on the water, mountains for skiing close by. I can see us there. Yeah, let's go for that.'

'Dan, I don't think she's going to ask.'

'She' turns out to be the sister in charge, tall, unsmiling, brusque in manner though not unfriendly. Her name badge reads: LYDIA. She shows us to the far end of the ward. I can feel Doggo shift and squirm in the backpack as we run the gauntlet of comatose patients, almost as if he senses the presence of people hovering on the fringes of life, kept from death only by the machines stacked around them. The hum and hiss of ventilators is broken by a staccato symphony of beeps from the monitoring equipment.

The place is manned to the hilt, and I'm thinking there's no way in the world we can whip out a dog without one of the nurses spotting us when, thankfully, Lydia shows us into a room with only one bed.

'We try and give them a bit of privacy at the end if we can.'

'How long?' asks Edie.

'Soon, although your grandmother's a fighter. She was unconscious when she got here, but you learn to tell what they're like, to read the signs.' She glances at the monitors. 'It's all up there. She doesn't want to let go.' She gives a warm and unexpected smile. 'I'll leave you alone with her.'

Geraldine doesn't look like a human being; she looks like something spat out by the sea, cast up on the shore – a piece of driftwood weathered back to its toughest knots and sinews and bleached by the sun. This impression is reinforced by the rhythmic ebb and flow of the ventilator, like waves breaking softly on the sand. It's easy to look beyond the plastic valve in her mouth, to ignore the many tubes, wires and cables running in and out of her, and see that she was once a beautiful woman.

I unshoulder the backpack and lay it on the end of the bed. Releasing Doggo, I immediately clamp my hand over his muzzle. 'Ssshh.' He understands – what doesn't he understand?

– and yet when he sees her lying there, he can't help letting out a tremulous whimper. He treads carefully towards her and licks her cheek several times. Then he buries his snout in her neck, just below her right ear, and pushes hard. And again. Trying to stir her, force her back to consciousness. I know it's not going to happen; she's too far gone. I turn to Edie, who reads my pleading look and shakes her head. *You're wrong*, say her eyes. *It wasn't a mistake.*

Doggo barks twice in frustration before I manage to calm him, silence him. I think we've got away with it, but a few moments later the door swings open. Lydia's quick, appraising look takes in Doggo sprawled over Geraldine. 'What on earth do you think you're doing?' she hisses. 'Get it out of here.'

'They only had each other,' pleads Edie.

'There are rules!'

'And there are some things bigger than rules.'

Lydia's having none of it, though. 'I'm calling security.'

Fortunately, she casts a parting glance at Doggo, because it stops her dead in her tracks. He's staring at her, his dark eyes utterly bereft, without hope. I don't hear it at first – my ears aren't trained to such things – but Lydia's are. Her eyes flick to the heart monitor. It's nothing dramatic, a slow ascent: 53 . . . 54 . . . 55 . . .

Even Doggo is staring at the monitor now, but probably because we all are. 58 . . . 59 . . . 60 . . .

Edie is the one who spots the movement. 'Her hand . . .'

A twitch. Something. Nothing. But there it is again, a sort of spasm in the desiccated claw. I take the hand, as light and fragile as a fledgling bird, and gently lay it on Doggo's head.

61 . . . 62 . . . 63 . . . 63 . . . 63 . . .

I could swear he's emitting a long, low sigh when the alarm goes off. I just have time to register the flatline on the monitor before Lydia hurries over and flicks a switch on the machine, killing the piercing wail. Doggo doesn't seem to understand what has happened until the ventilator is also turned off and he no longer feels the rise and fall of the bony chest beneath him.

We all look at him lying there, stuck to her, almost as still as she is. For a horrible moment I think he's going to will himself after her, down the same dark road, but when I run my hand from his head to his hindquarters, he looks up at me.

I can hear Edie sobbing gently behind me and I don't want to turn because I know I'll lose it too.

'This never happened,' says Lydia. Even in the subdued lighting of the room I can see the sheen in her eyes.

'Thank you,' I say.

She turns at the door. 'Who are you really?' Before I can trot out the lie, she shakes her head as if to say, it doesn't matter.

Chapter Twenty-Four

I HAVE TO CARRY Doggo up to Edie's flat.

'It's weird, he seems twice as heavy as usual.'

They're about the first words I've spoken since the taxi picked us up at the hospital. I can't imagine what the driver made of us – Edie and I in sombre silence on the back seat, shoulder to shoulder, with Doggo laid across our laps like an old picnic blanket.

Doggo gets the sofa and the fillet steak that Edie had planned for her own dinner. I'm ravenously hungry, and when he refuses to eat, I demonstrate what's expected of him.

'Hey,' chides Edie. 'I can whip something up for us.'

We get cheese soufflé and a green salad, which we eat by candlelight at the small circular dining table.

'I've never seen anyone die before,' says Edie eventually.

'Me neither.' I lay my fork on my plate. 'It didn't seem like dying, more like she just floated off somewhere else.'

'Like a balloon.'

'Like he gave her a little nudge and off she went.'

Edie glances at Doggo curled on the sofa. 'I really don't think he should be moved, not tonight.'

'No?'

'Stay,' she says.

'I can crash on the sofa with him. Do you have a blanket?'

'Sorry, no blankets. You'll have to come in with me.' She smiles. 'I promise to keep my hands to myself.'

'If Tristan finds out . . .'

'He won't. And it's a chance to fine-tune our pitch.'

What with the events of the past few hours, it has completely slipped my mind: we're presenting our take on the Vargo TV ad to Ralph and Tristan tomorrow afternoon.

We lie there on our backs in the darkness, she in a T-shirt and knickers, me in my boxer shorts (no shirt, because I'll only crease it and I've got to wear it again tomorrow). We do indeed discuss our pitch, refining it, coming up with a couple of additional slick phrases of the kind that will appeal to Tristan. It's not late, but we're both drained, and I can feel myself beginning to drift off. I keep dragging myself back from the brink, wanting to stretch out the pleasure, to revel in the strangely suppressed intimacy of staring at the ceiling together.

'I'm glad it worked out.'

'What's that?' she asks.

'The job.'

'Me too. Everyone is. You've gone down well with the troops.'

'Megan aside.'

'True.'

'She asked me for the recording yesterday,' I say.

'What did you tell her?'

'That I'd already deleted it.'

'Insurance?'

I only know I'm going to say it a split second before the words tumble out of my mouth. 'I lied to you too . . . about the lunch with my mother.'

She turns her head to look at me. 'Oh Dan, you poor thing.'

'No, it's okay.' The tremor in my voice suggests otherwise.

She swivels on to her side. 'Who?'

I can't give her a name because I don't have one. I tell her everything else I know, though, calmly fielding her questions. When I'm done, she slips out of bed and closes the door.

'I'm not sure he could take it in his current condition,' she says as she slides back beneath the duvet.

'What's that?'

'Here, I'll show you.'

She wriggles closer, and a moment later I feel the soft, searching pressure of her lips on mine.

Chapter Twenty-Five

G OD ONLY KNOWS what Doggo makes of it all. He has witnessed me sleep with three different women in little more than a month. I want to tell him that three women in four years is a much more accurate indicator of my sexual promiscuity.

He's better this morning, though not by much, just enough to wag his tail weakly when I dump myself next to him on the sofa. I'm still not convinced we did the right thing. Yes, he got to say goodbye to his beloved Zsa Zsa, but what consolation is that to a dog? I'm not sure they appreciate the finer points of closure.

We've been sitting solemnly beside each other for ten minutes when Edie appears, padding down the corridor in bare feet and a T-shirt that's just too short to conceal everything.

'Morning, boys.' Her voice is still husky with sleep.

'Oh God, look at you . . .' I say, winded by a sudden stab of desire.

She kneels in front of us and kisses Doggo on the top of his head. She then takes my face in her hands and kisses me gently on the lips. 'Coffee?' she asks.

'Sounds good.'

'Toast?'

'I don't do toast.'

'Well I do.'

She also does freshly squeezed orange juice and ripe mango. Doggo gets a tin of tuna mashed up with some bread that's been soaked to a pulp in milk. It's good to see his appetite has returned. Given how little I've slept, my head should be thrumming with exhaustion, but I feel remarkably alert, as if someone has turned up a secret dial on all my senses. I watch Edie going about her business in the kitchen and I wonder if I'm observing a routine that will one day be a part of my life. I'm entitled to hope, at least a little, after what she told me in the early hours of the morning.

'I haven't slept with Tristan since the first time we met.'

'Hmmm?' I grunted, half asleep.

'I think I knew even then that I wanted to be able to tell you that one day. Now I have.'

'I had no idea.'

'That's because I was scared.'

'Scared?'

'About what I was feeling. About Clara coming back. And I could see you weren't ready, which isn't surprising after what she did to you. So I waited. I didn't mind. It was good for me, a kind of penance. Let's face it, I haven't exactly been a good girl. I only wavered once, after the wedding.'

'The wedding?'

'When Barbara said you told her you could never have a relationship with a co-worker because it would be too claustrophobic.'

'That was confidential. She told you that?'

'Not me – my mother. They're old friends.'

'Edie . . .'

That's when she pressed her finger to my lips, silencing me. 'No, don't. I understand. And I think you're right. I'm not sure I could either. But at least we know now.'

'What?'

'Just how good it could be if we didn't work together.'

'But I love working with you. I love the bus ride in every morning, knowing I'm going to be seeing you soon, wondering what you'll be wearing.'

'You notice what I wear?'

'Sure.'

'Good,' she said.

Time is tight. We shower separately, significantly, as if already rehearsing for the charade we're about to play out. Edie offers me a shirt from her closet. Douglas left it behind when he moved out, and although it's not exactly me (I don't do stripes, or stitched detailing for that matter), it's better than showing up for work in the same one I wore yesterday. That's the sort of thing that might not be missed by eagle-eyed Margaret in Accounts.

There's no park near Edie's place, so Doggo does his morning business on the pavement right by Pimlico tube station. I bag it and bin it, which is when Edie suggests it's probably best if we part company now. A couple of people at work live south of the river, not least of all Tristan, and she sometimes bumps into them on the Victoria Line through to Oxford Circus.

'Don't worry,' I say. 'We'll jump on a bus.'

'You can take the 88 from right over there.'

Hordes of weary commuters are streaming past us into the station. I can sense a public kiss is out of the question, so I offer my hand and say with mock formality, 'Thank you, that was a pleasure.'

She smiles. 'Indeed it was.'

Chapter Twenty-Six

M EGAN HAS BEEN pleasingly subdued, even withdrawn, since the Turdgate incident. The prospect of the pitch later seems to have brought her back to her loud, uninhibited and generally insufferable self. I can smell the bullish confidence coming off her. I suspect she wants us all to smell it. She's a boxer strutting her stuff at the press conference before the fight, looking to unsettle her opponent, score a psychological point or two.

The meeting is set for noon, and whether it's Megan's doing or just simple nerves, Edie suddenly decides to rework all our storyboards beforehand.

'They're not strong enough.'

'Edie, they're fine.'

'Exactly. Fine. But no more than that.'

I don't put up too much of a fight; it's a chance to sit beside her at her desk, to press my thigh against hers, to breathe her in while she sketches away. We're interrupted after an hour by Josh. He's so excited he can barely speak.

'They went for it. The cartoon. They want it!'

'Who?'

'*Private Eye*.' They don't just want it; they want more of the same. They think it can be a comic strip: a study of the lives of well-meaning liberal thirty-somethings through the eyes of their worldly-wise pet. 'The dog was the clincher. They love the dog.'

We turn as one and look at Doggo, whose head is hanging over the edge of the sofa. 'Is he all right?' asks Josh, frowning.

'He had a tough night.'

It's not the time to celebrate or figure out what this means for Josh, Doggo and me, but I can sense a door opening. Well, not so much a door as an escape hatch.

With fifteen minutes to go, Tristan drops by the creative department to say that Ralph is still out so the meeting has been put back by half an hour. He looks at me in a strange fashion, as if puzzled by my presence, before asking me to join him in his office.

'Shut the door,' he says. 'Grab a pew.' I settle down opposite him.

'Nice shirt,' he observes.

'Thanks.'

'Where did you get it?'

The lie comes easily. 'It was a present from Clara.'

'Clara, huh? Must have been tough, her walking out on you like that.' There's something slightly manic in his eyes.

'It wasn't easy.'

'So you can guess how I'm feeling right now.' He leans forward in his chair. 'The thing is, I know that shirt, I've seen it before.'

'Where?'

'Don't fuck with me, Dan. You know where.'

I take a moment to weigh his words before replying as calmly as I can, 'It's not what you think.'

'Since when do you know what I think, my friend?'

'I'm not your friend, Tristan.'

'No, but you could have been . . . you *should* have been . . . because you're about to find out what it's like to have me as an enemy. You are *so* going down. Both of you.' I figure it's best not to answer but to stare and let him stew in his sneering contempt. 'What?' he asks eventually.

'You're a married man, Tristan.'

'Are you threatening me?'

'I'm just saying it would be unfortunate if your wife got wind of all this.'

He sizes me up with narrowed eyes. 'You wouldn't. A good person like her who's done you no harm? No, I don't see it, not someone like you.'

He's right; I wouldn't ruin her life, even believing I'd be doing her a favour. I spread my hands and ask casually, 'Are we done here?'

'We're very far from done. But yes, you can get the hell out of my office.'

'Shit,' says Edie, pacing around. 'He must have gone through my stuff when I wasn't looking.' She stops and turns to me. 'I'm sorry, I just didn't figure him for a snooper.'

I push aside the nauseating image of a naked Tristan rifling her bedroom closet while she takes a shower. 'It's only a problem if you want him back.'

Edie stops pacing. 'I didn't lie to you, Dan. I haven't wanted him from the moment you showed up in my life.'

Does she have any idea how good that makes me feel?

'Then we'll just have to weather the shit-storm together, won't we?' Edie looks grim-faced at the prospect. 'You're up and running with the SWOSH! account. He can't touch you.'

'You reckon?'

It's my cue to say something cheesily heroic, like 'I won't let him,' but I'm not sure I can prevent him wreaking a subtle and sustained revenge from the shadows once he has set his mind on it.

Tristan is all smiles and hail-fellow-well-met as we file into the conference room, although his eyes linger on mine just long enough to reinforce the threat he made earlier. I recall the first time I sat at the big oval table, when Tristan and Ralph (and Edie too, I suppose) first interviewed me, and I'm struck by a sudden sense of how much has happened to me in the intervening weeks. After years of benign inertia, and for reasons I can't quite identify, my life seems suddenly to have broken into a gallop. I'm a rider hauling on the reins, but also enjoying the heady mix of terror and exhilaration, the wind in my face. I feel as if nothing can touch me, at least not in the places that matter, and I'm not sure I've ever felt quite that way before.

Ralph is in a mischievous mood. It may have been billed as a brainstorming session, but he knows full well that he's pegged out a battlefield. 'Okay, let's see if you bastards are worth what I'm paying you.'

It's probably nothing, but he would usually say 'we' instead of 'I' out of respect to Tristan, and I can tell from the flicker in Tristan's expression that the same thought occurs to him.

Clive and Connor are first up. Paradoxically, the endless

hours of violent and foul-mouthed exchanges behind the closed door of their office have produced a softly-softly take. Their vision for the TV ad – told through Clive's storyboards, and accompanied by a mellow, synthy soundtrack they've brought along with them – is a slow-motion narrative of a young couple (our target market) cruising around in a Vargo. The central conceit is that the world outside keeps morphing into something new as they interact with the vehicle. When the heated seats are turned on, winter gives way to springtime, the sunroof retracts, and outside the trees miraculously sprout leaves. White blossom falls all around, turning to snowflakes as the air con is activated. And when a destination is tapped into the touch-screen satnav, they find themselves transported as if by magic to a wild clifftop location, where the giant orb of the sun is sinking into the sea, silhouetting an armada of ancient galleons in full sail. 'Vargo. Feel Free to Dream.'

Not quite there, but not bad, not bad at all. The deal is that we wait until everyone has presented before throwing the thing open to discussion, and I nod my congratulations to them. Megan doesn't. She's looking quietly confident as she and Seth take the floor. Their approach is way down the other end of the spectrum: a frenetic blitz of snapshots detailing the crazy weekend lifestyle of the Vargo's uber-hip owners: waking up in their funky loft apartment (done to death, or a homage to the seminal ads of the late 1980s, depending on how you look at it); tearing off to Borough Market, where the Vargo's spacious boot easily swallows everything from home-baked pies to bunches of flowers; communicating with friends via the hands-free Bluetooth as they weave through some attractively distressed parts of the urban jungle; then breaking out into the countryside, where the satnav guides them to their final destination – a remote spot on the banks of a tree-trimmed river. They set up an elaborate picnic for four (not two, note) while glancing expectantly downriver. And here's the twist – it's the River Severn, known for its tidal bore, and their friends (an equally attractive young couple, of course) turn up to join them on surfboards, riding the freak wave upstream. Cue lots of jollity and laughter, then a final crane shot at dusk of the four friends leaving in the Vargo, the surfboards strapped to the roof rails. 'Vargo. Why Settle for Less?'

It's a strange line, not up to Seth's usual high standards. Something sheepish in his look tells me that he might not have had much of a hand in it, or the concept for that matter, which Tristan now endorses with a hearty 'Bravo.' Whatever he thinks of our idea, I know he's going to grind it into the dirt with his heel.

We also have an attractive young couple, although in our scenario the woman is driving (Edie's idea). Cut to a close-up of her hands on the steering wheel: 'Leather Steering Wheel as Standard.' He punches their destination into the satnav: 'Satnav as Standard.' She flicks a switch: 'Heated Front Seats as Standard.' And so on – parking sensors, low emissions, stunning fuel economy, all as standard – until the final frame, which reads: 'Vargo. Because It's Good to Have Standards.'

Predictably, Tristan looks underwhelmed. He even manages to produce a slightly puzzled frown. Ralph kicks off the discussion with some words of encouragement and congratulation for all of us, although something tells me he's disappointed. Tristan is quick to say that for him the standout concept is Megan and Seth's, with its high-energy buzz and glamorous message.

"'Why Settle for Less?'" says Ralph, doubtfully. 'It lacks the punch of the visuals.'

'A little, maybe,' concedes Tristan. 'What about: "Why Settle for Water When You Can Have Wine?"'

Ralph gives a sudden loud laugh and turns to the rest of us. 'What do you reckon, guys? Alcohol and cars? Think we can get that one past the ASA?' He turns back to Tristan. 'That's the Advertising Standards Authority, by the way.'

Tristan knows full well what the ASA is, just as he knows he should have stopped to think before offering his opinion. 'Something like that,' he replies defensively.

'Orange juice,' suggests Ralph. '"Why Settle for Orange Juice When You Can Have Water?"' A brief pause. 'Nah, it doesn't have the right ring.' It's not just the heavy dose of sarcasm, it's the look of challenge in Ralph's eye. There's something serious in the air, and I'm not sure Tristan has any idea what it is. I do.

While Tristan bristles, Ralph drives the discussion forward. We're all missing something, something essential, and he can't quite put his finger on it. He's intrigued by the dream-like quality of Clive and Connor's approach, but ultimately it's just too mysterious, too vague and elusive. And although he likes the archness of our line – 'Because It's Good to Have Standards' – he's not sure that flogging a car on its gadgets and gizmos is the way to go. As for Megan and Seth, when you pin a product to a type of person through a lifestyle narrative, you run the risk of alienating whole swathes of the population.

'There's a danger they'll ask themselves "Why would I want to buy a car that's driven by arseholes like that?"'

'Arseholes?' says Megan, as if she's not quite sure whether she heard him right.

'Not to you, maybe.'

Condescending smiles come easily to Megan. She has also known Ralph for ever, which I suppose is why she feels entitled to say, 'Ralphy, you're more than twice the age of the people we're targeting.'

'Don't I know it,' he replies. 'But I can still spot a smug, loft-dwelling prat at fifty paces . . . *Brute*.'

You don't need to be an expert on Shakespeare's *Julius Caesar* to get the gist of what he's saying. *Et tu, Brute?* She has betrayed him, and he wants her to know that he knows.

I'm not sure what triggers it − maybe it's the crackle of barely contained aggression in the air, the sense of something about to turn seriously nasty − but I have a sudden vision of the shaven-headed thug in Athlone Gardens insulting me ('you doughnut') and Doggo ('Quasimodo') from his perch on the brick balcony. That's when the line pops into my head.

'Give me a minute,' I say, leaping to my feet.

There's relief around the table, because anything is better than what's about to kick off.

'Huh?' says Ralph.

'Not even. I'll be right back. Talk amongst yourselves.'

The last thing I'm aware of before leaving the room is Edie's pleading look. *Don't leave me here alone*, it says.

What with Doggo still feeling out of sorts, I've left him with Anna in reception. She has him on her lap and is guiding his paws around her computer keyboard.

'Finished already?' she asks.

'Not quite. I need him.'

'But he's tweeting.'

'Later,' I say, scooping him up.

I've been gone no more than thirty seconds, and if they've been talking amongst themselves during my absence, you wouldn't know it from the leaden silence that greets me when I return with Doggo in my arms. I place him in the middle of the conference table.

'What do you see?' I ask.

'A dog eating our biscuits,' says Connor. (A man committing career suicide, says Ralph's tight smile.)

I remove the plate of biscuits and hand it to Edie. Doggo looks seriously annoyed.

'Honestly. What do you see?'

'Doggo,' offers Seth.

'No. What you see is a small and very ugly dog . . . possibly the least attractive dog you've ever seen.'

'Possibly?' enquires Megan with an arched eyebrow.

'Shut up, will you?' says Ralph. 'I think I know where he's heading with this.'

I drum my fingers lightly on the tabletop. Doggo pads over to me and I scratch his head and fiddle with his ears, and he's in heaven.

'Ugly can be lovable.' I look up at them all. 'Clive and Connor are selling a dream. Megan and Seth are selling a lifestyle. Edie and I, well, we're selling a bunch of bells and whistles. None of is us selling the car. We're embarrassed of it. But we don't need to be, because—'

'Ugly can be lovable,' says Ralph, intrigued. 'Got anything more concrete?'

'Only a line. It just came to me.' I hesitate, uncertain.

'Well?'

'The Hatchback of Notre-Dame.'

Seth laughs and slaps the table. 'Damn! And the French angle!' This earns him a withering look from Megan.

'It's just an idea.'

'No, it's not,' growls Tristan. 'It's a shit idea.'

'It's brave, it's risky, it's bloody genius.' Ralph turns to Tristan. 'It's everything this agency stands for, whether you like it or not.'

'Yeah, well me no likey.'

'Yeah, well we need talky.' Ralph turns to the rest of us. 'Go and grab lunch. Come to think of it, take the rest of the day off.' We're all getting to our feet when he adds, 'Not you, Megan – you stay.' I've seen Megan look a lot of different things since I arrived at Indology, but I've never seen her look worried before.

The door has hardly swung shut behind us when Connor hisses in his heavy Irish brogue, 'Does one of yous want to tell me what the fuck was going on in there?'

I shrug. 'Anyone's guess.'

Back in our office, I tell Edie that it's just politics, that it'll play itself out. I also ask her what she wants to do.

'Go home,' she replies.

'Okay.'

'Your home.'

*

The weather has changed its mind in the past few hours; the sun has burned off the clouds and there's now a warm breeze blowing through the streets of Soho. We take a cab to the Dock Kitchen at the top end of Ladbroke Grove. Edie has never eaten there. Doggo and I have, many times; it's sort of our canteen. The converted wharf building overlooks the Grand Union Canal and has a large raised terrace where you can eat lunch beneath white sunshades. We both opt for the grilled mackerel. The glass of white wine hits home, reminding me just how little I slept last night. It's a short stroll back to the bed we both know is waiting for us.

I think at first that I must have forgotten to double-lock the door to my flat when I left it two days ago, but then I see the suitcase in the hall and my heart lurches.

She has been checking her emails at the desk in the corner of the living room, but now she stands and turns.

'Daniel.'

'Clara.'

I can tell from the clothes and the deft touches of make-up that she has made an effort to look her best. She's moving rapidly towards me when she spots Edie over my shoulder and stops in her tracks.

'This is Edie. Edie, Clara.'

'Nice to meet you,' says Edie.

Clara's eyes slide down to Doggo. 'Doggo . . .' she coos, crouching and extending her arms towards him. There's something hesitant in the wag of his tail as he trots over; yes, he recognises her, but he's also wary. 'Look at you, little man.' I see him dart a nervous glance at Edie as Clara smothers him.

'I can't believe you kept him. Is he still Doggo? Did you find a name for him?'

'I'll leave you to it,' says Edie.

Yes, do that, say Clara's eyes.

'At least have a coffee or something,' I suggest feebly.

'No, you two have a lot to talk about.'

'I'll see you out.'

'It's okay.'

But I do, accompanying her downstairs. 'Nice surprise,' she says in the stairwell.

'I'm sorry.'

'She's beautiful.'

'Edie, you don't have to worry.'

'I'm not worried. Why would I be worried? Your girlfriend of four years just turned up looking like she's stepped off a bloody catwalk.' She stops at the front door. 'She wants you back, Dan.'

'You don't know that.'

A shadow of disappointment falls across her face. 'Wrong answer. You were supposed to say you don't want her back.'

I want to say it, but the words won't come. 'Edie . . .'

But she's gone, down the front steps and along the street. I know Clara will be watching from the window and I can't face putting on a public spectacle for her.

I'm not too surprised by Clara's opening gambit when I return upstairs. 'She's a little young for you, isn't she?'

'We work together. She's my new partner at the agency.' Why am I making excuses? I don't need to make excuses.

'Working from home today? Hot-desking?'

'Trouble at t'mill. Afternoon off.'

'Daniel, I'm a woman, she's a woman. I know that look in her eyes. It's okay.' She steps towards me. 'Hold me.'

Just one more time, I tell myself, because I didn't get a chance to when she left. I wish it felt worse, but it's like slipping on an old glove, or a shoe that's been shaped by years of wear. 'I came straight here from the airport,' she whispers into my neck. 'I'm sorry, I really messed up.' And now she's clinging to me, sobbing softly. 'You have to forgive me. Please forgive me.'

The little devil crouched on my shoulder is telling me that four years can't be wiped out just like that, but all the pain and hurt she has caused me can be. There's no angel on the other shoulder, but there is Doggo.

He's not just watching from across the room, he's looking me hard in the eye, and although it's a flat stare, tough to interpret, there's something distinctly coiled, almost menacing, in the set of his shoulders. I smile feebly. He's having none of it. He stands there inert, as if carved from stone, my conscience, my guide . . . my guardian angel.

How can it have taken me so long to understand?

I see myself, steeped in a lazy cynicism, playfully ribbing Clara about Kamael. I see Fran, cute and caustic, taking me to task at my sister Emma's lunch party: *Maybe you're looking for halos and wings when you should be looking for other things.* And I see Zsa Zsa, bone-gaunt in her bed at the hospital, content at last to give up the fight and let herself go.

I gently release Clara and run my fingers through her hair, my thumbs beneath her eyes, smearing away the tears. I feel purged, stripped of all ill-will towards her. I'm free to love her again, just not like before.

*

'It's me,' I say into my phone.

'I can see that,' replies Edie.

'I thought you'd want an update.'

'Not particularly. Not after the way you behaved.'

'Remind me, what did I do wrong?'

'You should have kicked her out for breaking and entering.'

'Entering,' I correct her. 'She had keys.'

'You should have changed the locks.'

'You're right, I should have, but I really didn't think she was coming back.'

'And now she has.'

'And now she's gone again.'

'Where?' asks Edie tentatively.

'I don't know. I didn't hear what she said to the cab driver.'

There's a brief silence. 'Where are you?'

'Sitting on your doorstep with Doggo and wishing you were here.'

'Don't move,' she replies, killing the call.

She's wearing denim shorts and a Pink Floyd T-shirt that's so threadbare it can only have been her father's. I can tell from her eyes that she's been crying.

'What happened?'

My hand goes to my cheek. 'This? Oh, she slapped me.'

'Good, it means I don't have to.'

'Go ahead if you want. It's still so numb I won't feel it.'

Edie peers closer. 'God, she really caught you. Has she got a ring on her middle finger?'

'She was pretty furious. She even tried to walk off with Doggo, said technically he was still hers.'

'What happened?'

I look down at Doggo. 'Tell her what you did, Doggo.'
He peers up at us, shamefaced.
'He didn't!' gasps Edie. 'He bit her?'
'More of a warning shot. No blood. Well, not much.'
Edie scoops Doggo up into her arms. 'Oh Doggo, my hero.'
He licks her face, as happy as I've ever seen him.

Chapter Twenty-Seven

I COULDN'T SAY HOW many times I've changed my clothes since Edie first woke me with a kiss and a cup of tea. I've done the full-blown suit (borrowed from J), the casual jacket (bought especially from Selfridges) and the V-neck jumper; I've done them all with collared shirts and ties, collared shirts without ties, and with any number of different T-shirts underneath. I finally settled for a button-down shirt and crew-neck jumper combination, only to change my mind as I was leaving the flat.

That's why Doggo now finds me walking beside him in jeans, suede chukka boots and a navy blue polo shirt. 'Eurotrash banker in weekend mufti' is how J described the look. It'll have to do, because he then shut the door of my flat in my face and locked it. Only Edie waved us off from the balcony. She mouthed something that looked suspiciously like 'I love you,' although I know she'll deny it later.

We should probably have jumped in a cab, but it's not so far on foot and I fancy a walk through Holland Park. I don't suppose it really matters if we're fifteen minutes late.

I never used to walk anywhere. It's another thing I've got from Doggo. He loves it more than ever, trotting along at the end of his lead, soaking up the sights and smells of the city. For me it's an opportunity to daydream or, like today, gather my thoughts.

I can't help feeling I should be more upset by yesterday's news that we didn't win the Vargo account. According to Ralph, they wavered, vacillated, almost took the plunge, but in the end the notion of selling a car by actively embracing its unfortunate appearance proved to be a step too far. We still don't know who they went with. Whoever it is, Tristan will no doubt be delighted, wherever he is. The last I heard, he tried and failed to get his old job back at *Campaign*. I can't imagine he cares too much. He's like a cat – he'll always land on his feet. I wouldn't be surprised if the next I hear of him his book is a massive best-seller and he's making a mint from speaking engagements. In some ways, I hope that happens. Given how he's put together, success is very likely to slake any thirst for revenge.

I still feel the odd stab of guilt about the part I played in his downfall, but that's probably because Ralph can't stop thanking me for alerting him to Tristan's master plan. I don't know the exact details of what Ralph did with the information, but it was clearly enough to head Tristan off at the pass with the board of directors, and ultimately see him ousted in a counter-coup. Megan, Ralph's longest-standing employee, also fell victim to the purge, having sold her soul to the young pretender. *Et tu, Brute.*

Indology is a far happier ship with both of them gone; that was clear to me even before I left. It didn't feel like leaving. I'd hardly been there any time at all. Besides, Doggo and I are always poking our heads in. Edie sometimes insists on taking him to work, and the office gets its postman back for a day. He likes a captive audience, which is slightly concerning given how much more attention is about to come his way.

The cartoon strip is up and running, beginning to make waves, well, ripples anyway. Josh and I struggled to find a title for it, and it still rankles slightly that he nailed it ahead of me, the supposed wordsmith. It's called 'Waiting for Doggo'.

One cartoon every other week can hardly be described as full-time work – even less so for Josh, who hasn't given up the day job at Indology – but when I'm not toying with ideas, building up a storehouse for the future, I'm working on my novel. Money will become an issue if the book doesn't find a home. At worst, I have an open offer from Ralph for a part-time consultancy role.

Edie, meanwhile, is flying high with her new copywriter partner. Seth has blossomed since Megan was forced out. Even he didn't realise just how close he'd come to total psychological collapse after nine months in a confined space with her. I worry less about the torch he has always carried for Edie since he struck up a relationship with Anna on reception.

Doggo stops to irrigate a small sapling on the south side of Holland Park. I'd follow suit if I thought I could get away with it; that's how nervous I am. We cross Kensington High Street and take the narrow lane leading to Edwardes Square.

I've only been here a couple of times before, to meet friends at the pub in the south-east corner, but I know exactly what to expect because I've checked out the house on Google Street View. It has four floors – the first two stuccoed, the top two of brick – and the iron balcony serving the long windows of the third floor is threaded with an ancient wisteria (dripping with purple flowers like bunches of grapes on Street View, but no longer in bloom).

I ease open the gate, cross the tiny patch of flagged front garden and mount the steps.

My heart is beating the most ridiculous tattoo in my chest as I look down at Doggo.

'Ready to meet my real father?' I ask.

He appears intrigued, even eager, and if he's up for it, then so am I.

My finger reaches for the brass doorbell.

Mark's Top 5 Literary Pooches

Bull's Eye from *Oliver Twist* (Charles Dickens)
Poor brutalized Bull's Eye, an English Bull Terrier whose master, Bill Sikes, is surely Dickens's most vicious creation.

Lassie from *Lassie Come-Home* (Eric Knight)
Whatever you think of the endless film spin-offs, the story of this female Collie so doggedly determined to be reunited with her beloved Joe still hits the spot.

Snowy/Milou from 'The Adventures of Tintin' (Hergé)
Do the Tintin graphic novels qualify as literature? Of course they do. Does Snowy, Tintin's Wire Fox Terrier, a wry and sometimes cynical observer of his master's travails, deserve a place on this list? Of course he does.

Belle from *Belle and Sebastian* (Cécile Aubry)
As a kid, I watched and loved the dubbed French black-and-white TV series that fed off the novel. Set in the Alps, it's the story of the improbable friendship that springs up between Belle, a wild Pyrenean Mountain Dog, and an orphan boy called Sebastian.

Montmorency from *Three Men in a Boat* (Jerome K. Jerome)
The full title of the novel is *Three Men in a Boat (To Say Nothing of the Dog)*, the dog being a Fox Terrier called Montmorency – hater of cats and kettles – who accompanies the three hopeless (and hapless) friends on their boating trip up the Thames to Oxford. Sublime stuff.

Reading Group Questions

1. After finishing the novel, what do you feel is the meaning of the epigraph in relation to the rest of the text?

2. Do you agree with the the reviews that suggested *Waiting For Doggo* was 'chick-lit for men'?

3. What were your first impressions of Clara from her letter? How did you feel about her return?

4. Did you warm to Dan as a character? At what point did you feel this began?

5. Pick out the most humorous moment in the novel for you.

6. How do you feel Doggo influences Dan? Have you ever experienced this with a pet?

7. How do you feel the theme of abandonment is represented in the novel?

8. How was the world of advertising presented to you? Do you believe this to be accurate?

9. How did you feel family was represented in *Waiting For Doggo*?

10. As the first person voice, do you read Dan as an reliable narrator?